# A Fine Fix

A Trudie Fine Mystery

by

Gale Deitch

*to Janet ~*
*Enjoy !*
*Gale Deitch*

Rosedale Press

A Fine Fix
First Edition
Copyright©2013 by Gale Deitch

NOTE: The recipes contained in this book are to be followed exactly as written. The publisher is not responsible for your specific health or allergy needs that may require medical supervision. The publisher is not responsible for any adverse reactions to the recipes in this book.

Rosedale Press Trade Paperback ISBN: 978-0-615-84664-4
www.gdeitchblog.com

This is a work of fiction and should be treated as such. Names, characters, places and incidents either are the product of the author's imagination or are used fictitiously, and any similarities to persons living or dead, real or imagined, are purely coincidental.

Cover Design: www.earthlycharms.com
Author's Photo: Holly Callen Berardi

To Stanley, my rock and my biggest supporter.

*"The only time to eat diet food is while you're waiting for the steak to cook."*

Julia Child

# Chapter One

When you hire Trudie Fine, you get the whole enchilada. Which is exactly what our clients got when my partner Zachary Cohen and I commandeered the stark stainless steel kitchen of a stately brick house in Embassy Row, filling it with spicy aromas and hot, festive colors.

My signature purple apron with orange polka dots draped snugly around my ample form, and the matching headband kept my black bob tucked securely behind my ears. As I chopped peppers and onions, jalapeños and cilantro, preparing salsa for the Schwartzes' backyard Mexican fiesta, I sighed at my plump, dimpled hands that rocked the Santoku knife back and forth across the cutting board. You'd think with all the slicing and chopping I did, at least my fingers would be svelte.

I was keenly aware of the contrast between my partner and me: Zach, a lean six-foot-two with a head full of dark curls, and me, round and full-figured and an entire foot shorter. My friends and family have always told me I have a "pretty face" and warm brown eyes, but today, on this steamy Saturday in July as I wiped the perspiration from my forehead, I had my doubts.

Zach carried baskets of tortilla chips outside just as Dana Schwartz clicked her way into the kitchen, her high-heeled sandals slapping the soles of her feet with each step. "Mel, are you in here? Melvin! Trudie, have you seen Mr. Schwartz? I've been searching everywhere for him." She pulled her iPhone out of her pocket. "Never mind. I'll just call him. I bet he's in the media room watching the ballgame."

Mrs. Schwartz resembled a scarecrow in her white linen, cropped pants outfit, her neck and limbs thin as broom handles and bedecked with layers of gold and diamond bling. Her short and spiky platinum hair stood out against her skin, which was burnished to a mahogany color.

"I saw him earlier. Maybe thirty or forty minutes ago. He came through the kitchen and went out on the patio to show the band where to set up the amplifiers."

"Maybe he's watching TV in the pool cabana," Mrs. Schwartz went on in her husky voice. "Tell me, Trudie. What was he wearing? The clothes I put out for him are still lying on the bed."

"Let me think." I glanced at the ceiling. "Oh, yes. Very snazzy. He has on a pink shirt with bright green palm trees and hula girls." To tell the truth, I thought Mr. Schwartz looked adorable.

She scowled and scrutinized me with obvious doubt about my own taste. "Tacky, tacky, tacky. I'll kill him." She extracted a cigarette from the kitchen drawer and held it between her bony fingers, displaying a glittering rock the size of a garlic clove. "He loves that unsightly shirt. I told him 'not tonight of all nights when everyone who is anyone is coming.' And there he goes putting it on anyway."

She plopped onto a stool, shaking her head, the frosted spikes stiff as beaten egg whites. "Trudie, I need a drink."

"Sure. Water?"

"Water is not a drink."

"Why don't we start you off with a nice glass of sangria?" If anything would calm Mrs. Schwartz, I knew my knock-out sangria, with the apples and orange slices that had been marinating in red wine for the last several hours, would do the trick. I dipped a ladle into the punch bowl, filled a glass and handed it to her.

After a few sips, Mrs. Schwartz sighed. "You know. That shirt is one of Melvin's favorites. I guess it will lighten the mood tonight, maybe break the ice."

"Sure it will," I said. "Especially with those coral pants. They picked up the color in the hula girls' leis perfectly."

"Coral pants!" She slammed down her drink and vaulted off the stool. "Melvin!" she shouted. "Where are you? You'd better hope I don't find you, because when I do, I will strangle you with my bare hands. Melvin!" She hurried out the patio door, heels clicking and soles clapping.

Zach walked in from the patio, peering back over his shoulder. "What was that all about?"

"Believe me, you don't want to know." I checked my watch. "Okay, Zach. Twenty minutes until party time. I'll get the margaritas going. If that new bartender isn't here soon, you're going to have to work the bar. We've never had trouble with this agency before." I revved up the blender and boogied over to the refrigerator to retrieve the guacamole then nodded to the bowls of salsa. "Zach, put these out on the tables alongside the tortilla chips. Oh, and make sure all the plates, napkins and cutlery are laid out attractively—"

"Trudie, slow it down a few gears. We have time. Everything's organized." He pressed the off button on the blender and arranged the hors d'oeuvres tray with crab-stuffed jalapeño peppers and portabella quesadillas.

When I get hyper, Zach is the only one who can calm me down. I paused and took a breath. "I know. But this is our first full-priced gig. Did you hear that, Zach? No discounts. No coupons for first time customers. We're in business now for real, with a signed contract and a twenty percent deposit. These are real clients, not friends or relatives."

Zach raised his eyebrows at me.

"Okay, so they're Ally's parents."

He cocked his head.

"Okay, so she was my college roommate. But we're actually going to make a profit this time." After two years of children's birthday parties, family reunions, and business meetings that barely covered our expenses, I knew this job would get our catering company, *A Fine Fix*, out of the red.

I lifted my arms high and wide, Santoku and all, and threw my head back, singing, "We're gonna make it after all."

"Okay, Mary Tyler Moore." Zach grinned and shook his head. "All you need is a hat to fling through the air."

"But we are going to make it. I know it. Here we are practically in the shadow of the White House, and seventy-five of the most prominent, wealthy people in the D.C. area have been invited to this party." I shook the Santoku at Zach. "They are going to remember us. And next week or next month or next year they are going to call. Yessss!" I pirouetted on my eggplant ballet flats.

"Trudie, put down that knife before you hurt yourself—or me, for that matter—and give me a high-five." Zach put his hand up to meet mine.

I smiled and slapped his hand.

"I knew *A Fine Fix* would make it," Zach said, grinning down at me. "Always believed in you."

"Not me, Zach. Us."

Zach had been my best friend since childhood, coming to my house every day after school. At age six, we'd started with an Easy Bake Oven, adding our own ingredients, cinnamon or raisins or chocolate chips, to improve the little cakes baked by the heat of a light bulb. My constant pleading finally convinced my mother to let us cook in a real oven. Zach and I made after-school snacks for our friends and soon were cooking dinners for my parents. Together we concocted all kinds of gastronomic creations, experimenting with whatever herbs and spices we could find in my mother's pantry. For

Zach, I think our kitchen provided a warm and nourishing environment that his own parents, professionals who were never home, could not. For me, I just loved to cook—and loved to eat.

We'd had a plan. After high school, I went to Johnson and Wales, a culinary arts school in Charlotte, and Zach went to the University of Maryland to study business management.

I had no desire to work in a restaurant preparing the same menu items night after night, but rather to own a catering business where Zach and I could tailor menus to our customers, to their tastes. Now, at twenty-nine, my dream of opening *A Fine Fix* had become a reality, and I knew that Zach was as excited about tonight as me.

The doorbell rang.

"Zach, are all the nachos and chips out on the table? Are the citronella torches lit?"

As the guests arrived, Zach worked the bar while I wove through the crowd with a tray of hors d'oeuvres. I recognized some of the faces: a senator and two congressmen I'd seen in the press, a local TV news anchor, a socialite I'd often read about in the Style section of *The Washington Post*, and a best-selling author who wrote CIA thrillers.

Where the heck was that bartender? Right now, I didn't even have time to contact the agency to send someone else. We needed help so Zach could serve and I could be in the kitchen preparing the other dishes. Thank goodness the Schwartzes had volunteered their housekeeper to assist with the serving, clearing and washing up later.

"Patio" was probably a misleading name for the massive terrace at the rear of the Schwartz home. One might describe it more as tiers of entertainment space. The top terrace level ran along the entire back of the house and could be accessed not only from the kitchen, but also from the dining room, family room, and library.

Guests, dressed in cruise-like wear—flowing cotton dresses with sandals, khakis and polos with deck shoes—mingled over their cocktails on the top terrace and the lower level, just a few steps down. Interspersed on both levels were round tables where they would be seated later for their meal.

Below the second terrace sat the pool deck, complete with lounge chairs and lighted umbrellas as well as a canvas-draped cabana outfitted with a dressing room, sitting room, bathroom and shower. Colored lanterns festooned the pool area, and a Mariachi band, wearing multicolor ponchos and sombreros kept the mood light and competed with the low murmur of voices and tinkling glasses.

As the sun set, a mild breeze danced across the terrace, and I inhaled deeply and glanced around the patio once more for a last check. I noticed Mr. Schwartz holding out his hand to greet a guest, but the other man shook his head and kept his hand in his pocket. They leaned into each other with what appeared to be a heated discussion, their voices raised, but not loudly enough for me to hear their words. A woman approached, and touched the man's arm in a calming gesture. She smiled at Mr. Schwartz and leaned in for a polite kiss.

Mr. Schwartz gestured to someone across the lawn, and a young man in a white shirt and bow tie approached him. The bartender.

Finally, I thought, making my way over to him. Then I realized that Mr. Schwartz was asking him to do something, pointing him toward the house. Following his directions, the young man walked down an outside flight of stairs and entered a basement-level doorway. So much for help arriving.

With the party underway, I stepped back inside to assess the food. I'm not a person to brag, but I know which spices to use and how much. That night my highly evolved olfactory sense assured me each dish was seasoned to perfection. The Mexican lasagnas were heating nicely in the oven, the pollo asada almost done to its ideal moistness. I spent some time brushing the salmon fillets with a honey-chili glaze and setting the individual cups of flan into water baths, ready to go into the oven. It didn't hurt to be able to do all our cooking in the Schwartzes' Viking 60" dual oven. If my arms were long enough, I would have wrapped them around this stainless steel gargantuan and given it a big hug.

Outside, the Mariachi band played on, its violins and guitars singing and its trumpets blaring. I smiled to myself. Except for that delinquent bartender, everything was just perfect.

A woman's scream pierced the clamor of voices and music.

Then, silence.

I gasped. Could there have been a cucaracha in the food? Had someone spilled hot cheese nachos on another guest?

I rushed onto the patio. A crowd had gathered around the pool. Soft cries and questioning whispers lilted on the summer breeze. I scrambled down two levels to the pool deck and edged closer, rounding the crowd to get a better view. In the center of the pool floated the body of a man, face down, a rivulet of blood swirling from his head and the palm trees and hula girls on his shirt billowing to the surface.

# Chapter Two

The next twenty minutes felt like hours. At the insistent buzz of the front door bell, I left Dana Schwartz with another glass of sangria and a box of tissues, and went to answer it.

"Detective Daniel Goldman, Metropolitan Police," the man said, flashing his badge. "Are you Mrs. Schwartz?"

"No. I'm Trudie Fine, the caterer. Mrs. Schwartz is in the kitchen."

Outside, the ambulance sat in the driveway, and several squad cars had double-parked at the curb, their blue and red lights flashing, giving the neighborhood a disco-like feel. Uniformed cops streamed in behind Detective Goldman, while others navigated their way around either side of the house.

"What's all this?" I asked.

"Senator Davies called the station. He seemed to think an investigation was in order."

"Investigation? You mean like murder?" Why in the jalapeño would anyone think it was a murder? Obviously, poor Mr. Schwartz had some sort of heart attack or stroke and hit his head when he fell into the pool. When his body was discovered, two of the guests had jumped in and pulled him out. Their attempts at CPR just hadn't been successful.

Detective Goldman moved toward the kitchen. His eyes had that drowsy, just-got-out-of-bed quality, and I could tell he hadn't shaved.

"I'm not sure if Mrs. Schwartz is up to seeing you," I said, thrusting my hand out to try to hold the detective back and getting an unexpected feel of his well-toned six-pack.

Before I'd realized it, he'd grabbed my wrist and spun me around, bending my arm behind my back. The Santoku knife, which I didn't even realize I still held in my other hand, clattered to the floor. He spoke quietly into my ear. "Miss, don't ever do that again." I felt his hot breath in my hair, and a whiff of spearmint drifted by my nose.

"Hey, that hurts. I was just trying to give Mrs. Schwartz some time before you go in to question her. As you might imagine, she is distraught over her husband's death."

"All right." He loosened his grip on my arm. "We'll give Mrs. Schwartz a little time. But I'll need to interview her at some point tonight." He picked up the knife and handed it to a uniformed cop.

Detective Goldman gestured toward the living room. "In the meantime, let's start with you...Trudie, did you say your name was?"

"Yes." I rubbed my wrist and lifted my chin to regain my dignity. "I'm the caterer, Trudie Fine. *A Fine Fix.* Heard of us?" I pulled a business card from my apron pocket and handed it to the detective.

Stepping forward, I didn't notice the change from smooth marble foyer floor to plush living room carpeting, and lost my footing. Detective Goldman threw his arm out in front of me and around my waist to catch me from falling and pulled me up against him to steady me. His body felt solid and reassuring. I flushed at my clumsiness and peered up at him. The glimmer in his eyes and the slight grin told me he was enjoying my discomfort. He released me above the peach silk loveseat, and my body sank heavily into the sofa cushion.

Detective Goldman sat down across from me in a floral wing chair. He pulled a notepad and pencil out of his inside jacket pocket, leaned back and rested his ankle across his knee, waiting.

"Will this take long?" I asked. "I need to look after Mrs. Schwartz until her daughter gets here. What do you want to know?"

Detective Goldman tapped the eraser end of the pencil on his shoe, staring at me. His dark eyes bored into me, and I wondered if this was some kind of technique used to get suspects to confess. Suspect? I wasn't a suspect, was I? There hadn't even been a crime.

"Wait a minute. Shouldn't you be talking to the people out back by the pool, the ones who first spotted the body? Isn't that normal police procedure?"

I detected another glimmer in his eye and the beginning of a smirk at one corner of his mouth. "You think you're pretty knowledgeable about police stuff. Are you in the habit of catering crime scenes, Trudie?"

"Of course not. But I watch police procedurals on TV all the time. They always talk to the suspects closest to the crime scene first. Anyway, this isn't a crime scene. Is it? Who would want to kill Mr.

Schwartz?"

I must have appeared nervous, because he smiled and shook his head. "Not to worry. This is just a routine investigation. And yes, I've got men out there questioning people." Goldman's shaggy brown bangs fell into his eyes, and he smoothed them back out of his face, a boyish gesture I found kind of appealing. He needed a haircut.

In fact, his white shirt sagged beneath the well-worn navy jacket, and his khaki trousers could use a good pressing. A bachelor, I thought. I checked out his ring finger to confirm. Daniel Goldman. Definitely single, and by his name, definitely Jewish.

I hated myself for listening to my mother's voice in my head. "Is he Jewish?" my mother would ask hopefully whenever I met someone new. "Single?" Not that it mattered. Any guy's interest in me was only a ploy to get close to my thinner, cuter girlfriends.

Like now. I had this single, Jewish guy's attention, but for all the wrong reasons. Some things never changed.

"You can start by telling me what time you arrived at the Schwartz residence today."

"Four o'clock on the dot. The party was starting at seven, and I always like to give myself a full three hours of prep time."

"Who greeted you when you arrived?" He positioned his pencil over the notepad.

"That was Mr. Schwartz." Poor guy, I thought. I had met Mr. Schwartz only twice, once at the Johnson and Wales graduation and again at the opening of his daughter Ally's restaurant. But I'd never really spoken with him before this afternoon.

Today I had liked him immediately, an approachable man with a balding head and pear-shaped body, his stomach bulging under the Parrot Head t-shirt. Mr. Schwartz welcomed us in, patted my back as if I were an old friend and led us into the kitchen, making us feel right at home.

"He helped Zach and me unload the van."

"Zach?" Goldman's pencil was poised again.

"My partner. Zachary Cohen. We had a ton of food and utensils to bring in. We didn't ask Mr. Schwartz to help. He just did."

My eyes began to tear up. I couldn't get rid of the image of his dead body floating in the pool. "Maybe we shouldn't have let him help us. It might have been too much stress on his heart on such a hot day. Could it have been a heart attack?"

Detective Goldman's eyes softened. "That's exactly what we're trying to find out, Miss Fine. So I appreciate your cooperation."

So it's Miss Fine now, is it? I couldn't tell if he was being respectful or continuing with his sarcasm. Why did I even care what this detective thought of me? Mr. Schwartz died today, and here I was ready to choose wedding patterns.

He went on to ask questions about anyone who had come through the kitchen or anything I might have noticed by the patio. Then he dismissed me to attend to Mrs. Schwartz and asked me to send Zach to the living room for questioning.

The guests were corralled into other rooms for questioning. I glanced out the patio door and saw that the band members were being held at the poolside cabana.

A lone cop, supposedly guarding Mrs. Schwartz, stood by the stove shoveling in a mouthful of nachos. Mrs. Schwartz was slumped over the kitchen table, either fast asleep or intoxicated, her hand wrapped around an empty glass. I noticed that the punch bowl held considerably less sangria than when I'd first left the kitchen.

The front door opened, and I recognized Ally's voice. "Let me in. I have to see my mother. Mom, I'm here. Where are you?"

"In here," I called, walking toward the foyer.

Ally's eyes were red and puffy. She fell into my open arms, and I held on tight, murmuring into her hair. "Oh, Ally. I'm so sorry."

When she spotted her mother, she ran into the kitchen and knelt beside her, patting her back. "Mom," she sobbed. "It's okay. I'm here now." She shook her mother's shoulders lightly. "Mom?"

Mrs. Schwartz lifted her head, her eyes squinting against the light. "Allison. Is that you?"

Ally nodded, her eyes welling up.

"Oh, baby. Daddy's gone." Mrs. Schwartz lowered her head again and sobbed, her shoulders heaving.

"The detective wants to ask you some questions," I said quietly to Zach.

As Zach left the kitchen, he paused and put his hand on Ally's back. "I'm sorry," he muttered.

She turned to him and nodded.

I knew the two of them had a past together, but I wasn't sure where that stood. All I knew was that it had ended badly a few years before, and Zach had suffered for it. As had I. In all our years as friends, Zach and I shared everything. But that time he'd closed himself off and shut me out when all I'd wanted to do was provide him comfort and a shoulder to cry on.

The basement door opened, and the young man I'd seen earlier wearing the white shirt and bow tie emerged holding a bottle of wine. Probably in his early twenties, he was tall and tanned with hair a blend of colors from a rich caramel to a white blond and had the kind of chiseled features you saw only on the pages of a fashion magazine.

His hazel eyes darted from person to person, as if trying to make sense of the commotion in the kitchen. "Uh…I'm looking for Trudie Fine," he announced to no one in particular.

I swallowed hard. This Adonis was here to see me? "I'm Trudie Fine."

"Hi," he said, his face breaking into a smile, accentuating the cleft in his chin and exposing a set of luminous white teeth. "I'm Bradley Miller, your bartender."

# Chapter Three

I t was ten o'clock. Zach and I sat at the Schwartzes' kitchen table, held hostage with Bradley Miller, the agency bartender. Zach had been the one to use the words "held hostage." Personally, I wouldn't have minded being trapped on a desert island with Bradley. Every time he smiled, I was sure he could see the polka dots on my apron thumping wildly.

I saw the way Bradley and Zach watched Ally when she walked her mother upstairs to her bedroom. The same way all men regarded Ally, tall and thin and gorgeous with straight blonde hair. You'd think I'd be used to it by now.

According to her own rendition of the story, Allison Schwartz had been adopted, the product of a fifteen-year-old cheerleader who had gotten herself knocked up by the high school star quarterback. Hence, her gorgeous features.

Still, Ally and I got along well as roommates at Johnson and Wales. Apparently, she'd chosen me as the one person she could come to about anything, including her boyfriend problems. And she often took my advice. Ha! Me, who never even had a boyfriend. In return, she taught me how to maximize my best features with clothing and makeup. Unfortunately, nothing could cover up my double chin or my bulging derrière, which had already maximized themselves.

Unlike me, Ally studied restaurant management, wanting others to do the cooking while she controlled the money. After graduation, the Schwartzes bought their daughter her own restaurant, *Ally's Galley*, in Georgetown. They hired a chef straight from the Cordon Bleu and an experienced bar manager from New York. Ally handpicked the wait staff and host. The menu was haute cuisine, the ambiance exquisite and the grand opening a huge success with raves from food critics. Her restaurant soon was making money.

If I sound jealous, maybe I was. But only at first. Ally's wandering spirit caught up with her. She tired of handling the books and hired a business manager for his hunky looks and great ass and put all her energies into screwing him. To be perfectly blunt about it, eventually he screwed her and ran off with the profits. Ally could not convince her father to bail her out, and she had to close the restaurant.

"What I don't understand," Zach said to Bradley, "is exactly when you got here. And what were you doing in the wine cellar?"

Bradley flashed his white teeth at me again then turned to Zach. "I've already told the police. It was about eight o'clock. I didn't ring the doorbell because I was late and heard the band playing. So I walked around to the backyard. Most of the guests had arrived, and I headed to the bar. But you were already setting it up, Zach. That's your name, isn't it?"

"Yeah. That's me. But why didn't you tell us you were here?" Zach's outstretched hands asked for an explanation.

"Mr. Schwartz spotted me with my bow tie and signaled me over to him. He asked me to find a particular bottle of Spanish wine, a vintage Tempranillo, for one of the guests to taste." Bradley pointed to the bottle with both hands in a spokes-model gesture.

"But you would have had to come through the kitchen to go down to the wine cellar," Zach persisted. "Trudie would have seen you."

"Zach, I saw the whole thing," I said, finally able to pry my gaze away from Bradley. "Mr. Schwartz directed him to go into the wine cellar through the outside stairway."

"There's an outside entrance?" Zach asked. "Okay. So you're downstairs in the wine cellar." Zach was frustrated. I could tell by the way he shook his head and ran his fingers through his hair, trying to make sense of Bradley's story. "You're in the wine cellar for what…forty-five minutes? An hour? It's taking you all that time to find this bottle? And right outside, a woman screams, sirens wail and cops run through the house herding the guests from room to room, and you don't hear a thing?" Zach almost levitated out of his seat as he spoke.

I frowned. Zach had some good points. After all, we didn't know who this guy was. He could have disposed of the real bartender to get into the party. Could he have harmed Mr. Schwartz in some way?

That senator who had called the police suspected some kind of foul play that needed investigating. I scanned the room for my Santoku in case I'd need it for protection. What had that cop done with my knife? It had cost me more than the price of a steak dinner at Morton's.

Bradley leaned back in his chair, folded his arms and grinned. "Nope. Didn't hear a thing. Wine cellars have thick walls, and there must have been a thousand bottles down there. It took me a while to figure out his system, and I was determined to find this bottle if it took me all night." He turned his heart-stopping smile on me. "I wanted to make a good impression on Mr. Schwartz—the boss."

"Except," I said, pointing to myself and then Zach and trying to ignore my thumping heart, "I'm your boss, and Zach is your boss. The client is important, of course, but you report to us."

Bradley reached out and took my hand so that my finger now pointed to him. "I guess I didn't make a good first impression after all, Boss."

His eyes pleaded for mercy, and he brought my finger to his lips and kissed it. A tremor flickered through my body.

"I hope you'll give me another chance," he said.

"I wouldn't," a voice said.

I glanced up.

Detective Goldman glared at me, his eyes hard. Then he turned to Zach. "Mr. Cohen, I'd like to bring you in for further questioning."

This snapped me to attention.

"What? Bring me in where?" Zach's hair stood on end from running his fingers through it.

"What do you mean, 'bring him in for further questioning'?" I asked. "You mean to say you interviewed all those people, let them go home and Zach is a suspect? Is there some question of foul play?" As I spoke, I stood up and approached the detective but thought better of sticking my finger into his chest as I had initially intended.

"I didn't say anything about considering him a suspect. I just need to continue our conversation at the station. He was out on the patio a good part of the evening, both before and after the party began. He may have seen something important but didn't realize it at the time. And yes, foul play is always a possibility. Anyway, we need to let Mrs. Schwartz get some rest. So let's all get out of here."

"Excuse me?" I asked. "So you think foul play might be involved and you're going to leave Mrs. Schwartz and her daughter alone in this house tonight?"

The detective rolled his eyes. "I've got men stationed outside. And we've got the crime scene roped off. Nothing to worry about, Miss Fine." He gestured to Zach to follow him.

"Wait a minute. I need Zach to help clean up and load the van. I can't do this by myself." The housekeeper had been questioned and was so distraught over what had happened to Mr. Schwartz that the police had let her go home.

I surveyed the kitchen. Uneaten casseroles and bean dishes sat dried in their pans. A mixture of dirty and clean dishes, glassware and silverware were piled on every surface. The chicken, forgotten in the oven, had burned beyond recognition, and a charred scent hung in the air along with the charred remains of *A Fine Fix*.

"I'll help you," Bradley said. "That is, if you'll give me a chance to prove myself."

Zach stood by the detective, a bewildered expression on his face.

"Zach," I said, "As soon as we have everything cleaned up and in the van, I'll come down to the station to pick you up." I watched as Goldman led him out of the kitchen and waited until I heard the front door shut.

With Zach gone, I felt as if all the air had been sucked out of the room. Everything inside me, all my hopes and dreams, had deflated in an instant like a fallen soufflé. I took a deep breath.

"Okay, Bradley," I said, turning and handing him an apron. "Prove yourself."

# Chapter Four

In my purple apron, I must have resembled a grape Popsicle, frozen in the center of the Schwartzes' kitchen surveying the disaster around me. "Where do we even start?" I murmured, more to myself than to Bradley. After all, I was the professional. I'd cleaned up kitchens messier than this. Of course, I'd always had Zach with me. We were a team. I'd rinse and stack the plates, while he soaked the utensils in hot soapy water and lined up the stemware on the counter.

But Zach wasn't with me tonight. Zach was on his way to the police station for questioning. Why? Why Zach, the most trustworthy human being I'd ever known? My business partner, my best friend. Once, when I'd cut my finger chopping onions, he had cleaned the wound, applied a bandage and continued all my prep work. When the van's battery went dead late one night after I'd dropped him off at home, he'd driven to rescue me with his jumper cables. Tonight he was the one in trouble, and I couldn't even help him. Not even to be with him at the police station for support.

Here I was in the midst of ruins. Just a few hours ago, this job was our icing on a cake, our big break into the politically powerful Washington society. Now, who would hire *A Fine Fix* to cater their parties? Our company would only be a gruesome reminder of what had happened to Mr. Schwartz. I still couldn't believe it myself. This afternoon, Mr. Schwartz had been full of life, joking with Zach and me as he helped unload the van. He had greeted me with a warm bear hug, as if I were a member of his family. Why did the police suspect foul play? Who would want to hurt a man like Mr. Schwartz? Certainly not Zach.

"Oh, Zach." I began to tremble and covered my face, a loud sob escaping my lips.

"It's okay, Trudie." Bradley's voice soothed me as he put his hands on my shoulders.

"No, it's not okay." I shook my head, angry tears spilling down my face. "It's not okay that Mr. Schwartz is dead. It's not okay that Zach is at the police station. And it's not okay that tonight *A Fine Fix* has reached its expiration date and is ready for the garbage disposal."

Bradley's eyebrows creased together. "Trudie, you're going to sit down now and pull yourself together."

He turned me around, draped his arm around my shoulder, and escorted me to a kitchen chair. I turned my head toward him and breathed in the citrus and spice scent of his aftershave. I felt warm and safe, enveloped by his arm, and could have stood like that all night. He sat me down and handed me a couple of tissues from the box Mrs. Schwartz had been using. Then he ladled out a generous serving of sangria from the punch bowl.

"Here. Drink this."

I shook my head. "I never drink on the job."

He laughed. Gazing around the empty kitchen, he set the glass on the table in front of me. "I think it will be fine this one time."

"Thanks. You're not such a bad guy after all."

I took a big gulp and started to stand up. Bradley put his hands on my shoulders and gently pushed me back down. "You relax a while and let a pro take over." He slipped the apron I'd given him over his head and tied the back. Then he removed his bow tie, rolled up his shirt sleeves and dug right in to the sink full of dirty dishes, rinsing them and putting them into the dishwasher.

"A pro, huh? Let's see what you can do." For a guy with a drop-dead gorgeous face, I hadn't expected him to know how to scrape out one dirty pan, not to mention a whole kitchen full.

The sangria mellowed my mood. After a few minutes, I joined him at the sink and began drying and stacking the large platters, pots and pans. "You're pretty good at this. Where'd you get your know-how?"

He didn't answer at first, and I thought that maybe he hadn't heard my question. Then, concentrating his efforts on a sauté pan that already shone like a mirror, he blurted, "Many hours with my mom in the kitchen...watching her cry."

I stopped drying the pot in my hand. "Why was she crying?"

He put the pan in the drying rack and reached for another. He turned to me, opened his mouth and then closed it and shook his head. "My father was never around. Always with another woman." He dipped his head, but continued. "Not always the same woman, mind you,"

"She knew about those women?" I asked.

"We both knew. He wasn't very good at hiding his relationships. Truthfully, I think he wanted her to know. It was easier for him. He didn't have to work so hard at hiding his comings and goings. And when he finally left us, it wasn't such a big surprise."

I wondered why he was revealing so much to me. We'd only just met. "I'm sorry," I said, touching his arm.

When his muscles tensed, I pulled my hand away.

"I got over it long ago." He turned off the faucet and dried his hands on the apron. "Now can we change the subject?"

"Okay." I leaned back, my elbows resting on the counter. "There is something I'm curious about. Tell me, why is someone with your looks working as a for-hire bartender when you could be earning big bucks doing photo shoots for GQ?"

He turned to me, his eyes changed to a flat avocado green. He crossed the room to retrieve another stack of caked-on dishes and resumed his dishwashing with a silent vengeance.

Puzzled, I continued to stare at him. In my mind, I visualized a black-and-white print ad of Bradley on a sailboat, the wind whipping his hair, his eyes squinting into the sun. The apron he wore and the scouring pad in his fist just didn't fit with that vision.

"What?" I asked.

He glared at me. "I thought you were different, Trudie. I really thought you were the type to see beyond a person's appearance."

"Huh?"

"You don't know? You really don't know." His face reddened and the veins in his temples pulsed. "All my life, I've been judged by this face. Homecoming Prince, Prom King, Best-Looking Senior in the yearbook."

"So what's wrong with that?" If I had his looks, at least the female version of him, my life would have been so much easier.

"What's wrong with it?" His gaze shot to the ceiling. "This face gets me anything I want. And I'm not just talking about women. I'm talking about jobs. In a face-to-face interview with three candidates, I'm the winner every time. Waiting in line to get into a club, I'm escorted right through the crowd. In a busy restaurant, I always get served first."

He turned to me and wiped his hands again. "It's not right. Why should I be treated differently than anyone else? Why should my life be easier than yours?"

He turned back to the sink and began scrubbing furiously.

"Bradley." I threw the dish towel across my shoulder. "It's okay."

"People can't see to see beyond the surface." He took the sprayer and rinsed soap suds from a serving platter. "I just can't get away from that man."

"What man?"

As if someone had demi-glazed the air between us, everything appeared distorted.

"My father. I will never get away from him. I look in the mirror, and there he is."

"Bradley, listen to me. You are not your father," I said, beginning to understand.

"No, I am not my father. I don't want to use my assets the way he did. He destroyed my mother. He destroyed our family."

I was speechless.

"Why do I work for a bartending agency?" he continued. "I get hired sight unseen by the client. And hopefully, if a client requests me specifically, it's because I'm a good bartender, not because of my looks."

I nodded. My whole life, I'd been judged by my body, made fun of at school as Fatty Fine, always chosen last for kickball or relay teams, never invited to the prom. I'd always wanted to be pretty and thin and popular like the other girls, get invited to parties, asked out on dates. If someone as attractive and desirable as Bradley wasn't happy with himself, then my entire view of the world was skewed.

"I'm sorry. And I really do appreciate your help. I don't know what I would have done without you tonight. For what it's worth, I would hire you again in a heartbeat." I smiled. "And not because of your looks."

As he smiled back at me, his eyes returned to that Mountain Dew sparkle, and his dimple caused my body to go limp as a slice of cheese on a tuna melt.

AT ONE IN the morning, after two hours spent cleaning up, Bradley and I loaded the van and parted ways. I headed to the district station, located only a few blocks away. Thank goodness Detective Goldman had given me his card with the address or I wouldn't have known where to go. It had been a long day. I was running on watered-down consommé, weak and lifeless. But I had to get Zach. I pictured him sitting at a battered, graffiti-covered wood table, a bare light bulb dangling above his head and Goldman grilling him with questions. Maybe the detective had brought in another officer, and they were playing Good Cop-Bad Cop, trying to get poor Zach to spill his guts. Not that he had any guts to spill. I stepped down harder on the accelerator to make it through the intersection before the light turned red.

I pulled into a small parking lot behind the station and slid my van into a space next to a police cruiser, wondering if it belonged to Goldman. As I opened my door, I was tempted to bash it into his passenger door. Heck, the cruiser was white. My van was white. How could they trace me? Then I thought better of it. There were probably security cameras out here, and I needed to rescue Zach and get us both home.

I grabbed my purse. I might need bail money. But no, Zach was just there for questioning. Goldman wouldn't have arrested him. Not sweet Zach who didn't even like the violent act of tenderizing a steak with a mallet.

Maybe because this part of town, with all its embassies and wealthy home owners, didn't get much crime, the station was quiet and practically empty, only two of the dozen or so desks staffed at this hour of the night. I approached the officer at the front desk. He was leaning back in his chair working on a crossword puzzle, his feet propped up.

"I'm here to pick up Zachary Cohen. Where can I find him?"

The man shifted his eyes from the puzzle to me and motioned his head to the back of the station.

I spotted Zach sitting on a bench against the wall leaning forward, elbows on his knees and head in hands, fast asleep.

I sat down next to him and touched his arm. "Zach?"

His head popped up. "Wha...?"

"Zach, it's me. Are you okay?"

"Yeah, I'm fine."

"What kind of questions did they ask you? Why did they bring you down here?"

Zach peered down at the floor and shook his head. "Not now, Trudie. It's late. I need some sleep, and so do you. Can we do this tomorrow?"

"Sure." Something was wrong, but Zach had been through enough for today. For now, my questions would have to wait. "C'mon. I'll take you home."

As we stood up, Detective Goldman emerged from an office, his jacket draped over his arm. He grinned at me. "Well, Miss Fine. Nice to see you again so soon."

So I was Miss Fine again. "Sorry I can't say the same about you." I attempted to give him the "evil eye," a menacing glare that Bubby, my maternal grandmother, had taught me to execute when classmates mocked my plump figure. The tactic had kept them from bothering me, but this time, I wasn't sure if I really wanted to scare the detective away.

Goldman chuckled.

"What's so funny? Are you laughing at me?" I balled my fists and felt my face flush.

"No. Not at all." He continued to grin, his head tilted to one side as if examining me. "It's just that you've got this spunk, this fire inside you. Don't lose it."

No guy had ever spoken to me this way. I didn't know whether to take it as a compliment or to kick him in the shins.

The three of us left the station together and headed to the parking lot.

"You're not parked back here, are you?" Goldman asked.

"Of course I'm parked here. I had to pick up Zach, didn't I?"

"Didn't you see the sign, 'Authorized Vehicles Only'? Violators are subject to towing and a hundred-dollar fine."

"That's the most ridiculous thing I've ever heard. It's one-thirty in the morning, and there are only three vehicles in the lot. You knew I was coming to pick up Zach, so my van is an authorized vehicle." I huffed across the lot, pressing the button on my remote to unlock the doors, Zach following at my heels. I turned to the detective. "Besides, if I'd parked on the street, a young woman alone at this time of night, you probably would have had another crime on your hands."

"Clever defense, Trudie," he said. He stopped at the dark,

unmarked car a few spaces down from my van. Good thing I hadn't bashed the cruiser.

Goldman winked at me. "I do like that fire."

# Chapter Five

The ringing wouldn't stop. I heard it far in the distance. The sound moved closer and louder, and I realized it was my cell phone. I lifted my head, hoping it wouldn't split open like a melon, and squinted at the clock.

Seven o'clock. Who would be calling so early on a Sunday? I rolled to the edge of the mattress and reached for the receiver.

"Yeah," I grunted into the phone.

"Hello, Ms. Fine," the gravely female voice stated my name in an authoritative manner which had me sitting up at attention.

"Yes. This is Trudie Fine." My feet hit the floor and I trudged toward the bathroom.

"Barbara Lewis here. I was a guest at the Schwartz party last night."

The party last night. Oh, shitake. Memories of last night's events flooded into my consciousness—the body floating in the pool, the cops interrogating all the guests, Detective Goldman taking Zach to the station for questioning, and all the meticulously prepared dishes, dried up in their pans, burned in the oven. What a disaster. This woman must be calling to put me through the meat grinder.

All I could manage to squeak out was, "Oh."

"Oh is right," Barbara Lewis said. "Last night was just tragic. Poor Dana." She clucked her tongue.

I wanted to get this over with so I could get back into bed. "What can I do for you, Ms. Lewis?" Tucking the phone snugly between my jaw and shoulder, I opened the medicine cabinet, retrieved a bottle of Ibuprofen, and shook two of the small red tablets into my hand.

"Ms. Fine, I know this is late notice, but I'd like you to cater a small dinner party for me on Saturday night. Are you free?"

I froze, and the bottle fell out of my hand, pills skittering across the bathroom floor. Free? Sure I was free–for the next century. I scurried to the bedroom and grabbed my address book from the nightstand. "Let me consult my calendar a moment. Let's see," I ruffled the pages so the woman could hear. I didn't want to seem too eager.

"Yes. I just had a cancellation for this Saturday night," I lied, wondering whether I really wanted to take on a new job. Sure, our dream was to build a clientele from the gathering of prominent guests at last night's party. But that was before Mr. Schwartz died. Still reeling from the chaos of the night before, I wasn't sure if I was ready to face another catering job. Zach and I had thrown every ounce of ourselves into the Schwartz party, only to have it all thrown back at us. Our entrees hadn't even been served. We'd sapped our coffers of enthusiasm. Did we have anything left to take on a new gig?

On the other hand, this was our livelihood. Acquiring new clients from the Schwartz party had been our pie-in-the-sky goal. That's why I'd strategically placed our business cards at the bar and hors d'oeurves stations. Maybe this job was exactly what we needed.

Something wasn't quite right, though. "May I ask why you chose to call *A Fine Fix*? I mean, after last night's disaster." I slapped my hand to my forehead. Was I trying to sabotage my business?

"Ms. Fine, I am perfectly aware that your catering service was not responsible for that horrible tragedy last night. My husband and I absolutely adored the hors d'oeuvres. And the aromas coming from the kitchen were amazing. We were so disappointed that we couldn't sample all your dishes."

"Why, thank you, Mrs. Lewis." I said, flattered but not completely buying her reasoning. "We'll have to meet as soon as possible to plan your dinner menu. Do you have time this afternoon? I'll also need to see how your kitchen is equipped."

"Certainly," said Mrs. Lewis. "Let's make it two o'clock, shall we?" She gave me her address and phone number. "Oh, and bring that nice-looking assistant of yours."

My first inclination after hanging up was to phone Zach. He wouldn't believe that we had another job so soon. Then I remembered that I hadn't gotten him home until two in the morning. He'd had a harrowing evening, even more so than me. I would let Zach sleep a little longer, I decided, before I hit him with the big surprise.

IT HAD TAKEN all my self-control to wait until ten to call him with the news. He'd been as surprised and excited as I was.

Zach stood outside his apartment building when I pulled up in the little orange Honda Civic I'd driven since college. He appeared thinner and paler to me in the bright sunlight. Maybe the two of us should head to Ocean City for a couple of days. We could tan on the beach and take a stroll on the boardwalk where I would ply him with funnel cakes and cheese fries to put some meat on his bones.

"How are you feeling?" I asked, as he slipped into the passenger seat.

"Okay."

"What does that mean?"

"It means I'm okay."

"By 'okay' do you mean you're feeling good today or just 'okay' like tired and frazzled from last night?"

"Trudie, will you stop? I feel fine. Enough already."

"Do you want to talk about it? About the police station, I mean?"

He stared out the window. "Nothing happened at the police station. Goldman asked me the same questions he'd asked at the Schwartz house. What did I see when I set up for the party? Who was out by the pool? When did certain people arrive? That kind of thing." He turned to me but again wouldn't look me in the eye. "All right? Is my interrogation over now?"

"I don't understand why he had to drag you, of all people, down to the station if all he did was ask the same questions. It doesn't make sense."

I glanced at Zach, but he continued to stare out his window and didn't answer.

"Anyway," I continued, "let's be happy. We have another gig."

Zach's mood brightened at once, and he grinned. "I'm not sure which guest Barbara Lewis was, but I'm sure I'll recognize her when I see her. Anyway," he said, putting his hand up for a high five, "it looks like *A Fine Fix* is back in business."

After circling the block a few times, we squeezed into a space a block away from the Lewis' enormous red brick townhouse in Georgetown. Outside the massive wrought iron gates at the front entrance, I pressed a button and announced our arrival through the speaker. The gates opened and then closed behind us as we entered. A woman I supposed was the housekeeper stood waiting at the front door.

She seated us in what she called "the drawing room," which looked more like a living room to me. I wondered what the difference was. And what does one do in a drawing room?

Zach attempted to adjust himself on a chair that bore a close resemblance to a throne, its back reaching well above his head, with polished mahogany arms spaced too far apart for him to rest his own arms comfortably. I was directed to the "settee," a needle-point fabric sofa that left my short legs swinging above the floor. I crossed them at the ankles. We looked like toddlers trying to fit into an adult world.

"So nice to meet you both," Barbara Lewis said, extending her hand to each of us when she entered the room. Zach and I stood to greet her and then awkwardly readjusted ourselves as we sat back down.

I recognized Barbara Lewis right away as the woman who had calmed her husband and leaned in to kiss Mr. Schwartz at last night's party. Close up now, she appeared regal at almost six feet tall, having no trouble reaching the floor as she sat in the wingback chair that matched the settee. She wore a cream-colored Chanel suit trimmed with black braiding, her honey-colored hair swept into a chignon.

"I thought you were bringing your assistant," she said.

"This is my assistant, Zachary Cohen. My partner, actually."

"What about the young man with that nice smile?" She seemed disappointed.

"Oh, you mean Bradley, the bartender I hired for the party. If you'd like, I'll find out if he's available to work your dinner party as well." I did promise Bradley that I would hire him again, but I certainly would not mention why Mrs. Lewis wanted him there.

"See that you do. He was so eager to help when Melvin asked him to go down to the wine cellar to find that bottle of Tempranillo for Mr. Lewis and me. Such a pity we didn't get to taste it. That nasty business of Melvin in the pool."

Just thinking about the body floating in the pool, I shuddered. Zach and I glanced at each other, and I raised my eyebrows and nodded as if to say, "See, Bradley was telling the truth." I wondered what else our hostess had seen last night.

"Tell me," she continued, "Have the authorities discovered how he died?"

"I don't know," I answered, moving forward in my seat to try to reach the tips of my toes to the floor. "I believe they questioned everyone at the party, and I suppose the medical examiner needs to do an autopsy to determine the cause of death." At least, that's what they do on TV crime shows, I thought. "That usually takes time."

"Poor Dana," Barbara Lewis said, shaking her head. "I must call her to see if she needs anything." She crossed her legs and smoothed her skirt. "Now, let's get down to business. I'm planning an intimate dinner party for twenty on Saturday night. Let's say, seven o'clock cocktails and eight-thirty dinner. It must be elegant, but not decadent, and of course Mr. Lewis limits his carbohydrates."

"Of course," I repeated, scribbling notes in my day planner. I'd done the low-carb thing myself, and I knew exactly what to suggest. Barbara Lewis chose to start with cream of wild mushroom soup, charcoal-grilled, sliced London Broil with a duet of pureed root vegetables, sautéed Brussels sprouts, and brandy-poached pears with a cinnamon crème fraiche to finish.

Zach asked to see the kitchen and dining area, and Barbara Lewis led the way. The kitchen was a chef's dream, appointed with all the accoutrements of a commercial establishment. We wouldn't need to bring any cooking utensils except, of course, the knives that I always carried with me.

We paused as we passed through the butler's pantry. My heart fluttered at the display of several different china patterns, more than enough place settings in each design along with complementary silver and glassware. This job would be much easier than most because we wouldn't have to lug any equipment. The drawers contained an array of table linens in varying colors and fabrics, all with coordinating napkins.

The dining room was as big as my condo, with a table that could seat the President's cabinet and the Joint Chiefs of Staff combined.

We left with a promise to return the next day with a contract for Barbara Lewis to sign and to collect a twenty-percent deposit. Happy days were here again. Even Zach's disposition had improved. He smiled the entire way home. Well, until I mentioned stopping by the Schwartz house.

"Do you want to go with me?" I asked. "I want to see how Mrs. Schwartz is doing, and I barely got a chance to speak to Ally."

Zach's face fell. "I—I don't know. I wouldn't know what to say to them. We can't change anything." His voice jittered like a bowl of Jello. He shifted in his seat.

"Zach, what's wrong?" I put my hand on his. "You seem nervous. Of course it's going to be uncomfortable visiting them. Mr. Schwartz hasn't even been gone twenty-four hours. But Ally and her mother are going to need friends to rally round them and give support."

"I know. It's just that things like that are hard for me. But you're right, we should visit. Let's go."

I wondered what really made Zach so nervous. Why was he afraid to see Mrs. Schwartz? Or was it Allison? I knew Zach well, and I'd rarely seen him quite so disturbed. Maybe he knew more about last night than he would admit.

# Chapter Six

Graciella, the Schwartzes' maid, opened the door and led Zach and me through the house to the upper terrace, where Ally and her mother were lounging with tall glasses of iced tea. Both wore large Jackie-O type sunglasses and skimpy bikinis over their well-oiled, tanned skin. Ally's body was perfect as ever, curved in all the right places, and as firm and smooth as my top-scoring salmon mold in the Johnson and Wales final exam. Mrs. Schwartz, on the other hand, appeared skeletal, reminding me the bones left on the platter of Peking Duck Mr. Wu had carved at my table on my last visit to his restaurant.

It stunned me to find them here overlooking the pool where Mr. Schwartz's dead body had been found. Yellow police tape still ringed the perimeter.

"Trudie, dear." Mrs. Schwartz held out a hand to me. "How considerate of you to visit us. Come, sit down. You too, Zachary."

I took her hand and held it a moment. "I brought you some meringues." I extended the cellophane-wrapped platter of white-peaked cookies I had whipped up this morning while waiting to call Zach. Thinking about Mr. Schwartz's death and all the chaos that followed, I had beaten the egg whites with a vengeance. It had done wonders to relieve my stress.

"So lovely of you, Trudie. Graciella, please set these out for us all to enjoy. And refill the pitcher please, would you? We'll need more glasses."

Zach mumbled his regrets to Mrs. Schwartz and then pulled a chair up next to Ally.

"How are you doing, Mrs. Schwartz?" I stood above her. My body cast a shadow across hers as she peered up at me. "I'm so sorry about Mr. Schwartz. Such a wonderful man."

"Oh, Trudie. You don't know. You just don't know." She lifted her sunglasses and dabbed at her puffy eyes with a tissue. Then she pulled a cigarette from the pack on the side table, lit it, and inhaled audibly before lifting her head to release a stream of white smoke.

I turned to Ally and bent down to give her a hug. She wrapped her arms around me and held on, her body shaking with silent sobs. "I can't believe Daddy is gone."

"I know, honey. It's hard to believe." I stood up again. "He was so helpful to us yesterday, insisting on carrying in equipment from the van."

"He was my great, big, huggable, teddy-bear daddy," she said in a child-like voice. "That's what I always called him." She sniffled. "Come, sit with me, Trudie." She patted the empty space on her lounge."

I sat down on a deck chair, worried that if I set my butt on the side of her lounge chair, we would both tip over.

"Tell me," I said to Ally, noticing my own reflection in the huge lenses of her sunglasses. "What's going on with the investigation? Do the police know anything yet?"

She shook her head, her golden ponytail swaying back and forth, gleaming like corn silk in the sunlight. "Nothing. They can't even do the autopsy until tomorrow. Something about a backup in the morgue. Can you believe it?"

Graciella emerged with a tray, handed Zach and me our beverages and set the pitcher on the table along with the meringues, which she'd arranged on a silver platter.

"We can't even plan the funeral." Mrs. Schwartz held her palms up in helplessness. "People are asking, and I can't tell them a thing. Can't put the obituary in the *Post* yet either. I told Detective Goldman this morning he should know it's our law. Jews must be buried immediately, and autopsies really are not allowed unless absolutely necessary."

Her comment surprised me. The Schwartzes were not observant Jews, as far as I knew. Certainly not kosher, as there hadn't been an issue with my serving shellfish or meat and dairy together when Mrs. Schwartz and I had planned the menu for last night's party. In crisis situations, however, sometimes people revert to their religious beliefs. "I think there's some sort of petition you can file to block an autopsy, if it's for religious reasons," I suggested.

"Yes, Detective Goldman did say something like that. But I do want to find out how my dear Melvin d-d-died." Her bottom lip began to quiver, and a low, almost baritone, moan emerged from her throat, a sound I had never heard from a human being.

Mrs. Schwartz dabbed her eyes again and glanced toward the house. "Graciella, please bring that bottle of bourbon so I can sweeten my tea a little," she called then turned back to me. "Anyway, the detective said that a judge may deny the petition. When a suspicious death occurs, they usually insist on doing an autopsy. Goldman can't even push poor Melvin to the front of the line. Says he has to wait his turn.

"By the way, Trudie. I've left a check for you in an envelope on the kitchen table. It's the balance of what I owe you. Be sure to take it when you leave."

"That really isn't necessary, considering the food was barely touched." I was being polite by objecting. Zach and I could really use a boost to our account. The twenty percent deposit had barely covered our food costs, and we still had to pay the bartending agency for sending Bradley.

"Nonsense. You both worked very hard, prepared all the food and set up everything beautifully. What happened last night was not your fault, and you shouldn't suffer for it."

"Well, thank you. That's very kind." I was relieved but also ashamed to admit, even to myself, that despite the awful tragedy of Mr. Schwartz's death, I had worried that we would never get paid.

"Graciella," she yelled toward the house. "Where is that bourbon?"

The maid scurried out, the half-empty bottle balanced on a tray, one hand on the neck to keep it from falling. She poured a little in the glass, but Mrs. Schwartz grabbed the bourbon and, hand shaking, poured it into her tea until it almost reached the rim.

"What brought Detective Goldman here this morning?" I asked her. "Didn't he get everything he needed last night?"

"Evidently not." She took a long swallow of her tea. "For some reason he thought my head would be clearer this morning after I'd slept. I was perfectly lucid last night, wasn't I, Trudie?"

"You were...upset. What kinds of questions did the detective ask?"

"Oh, you know. The obvious. He asked if Melvin had heart problems. Oh no. I told him Melvin used to brag about how strong his ticker was." She laughed. "The only thing we had to be careful with was his severe allergy to peanuts."

Mrs. Schwartz had informed Zach and me about her husband's allergy. We'd been especially careful when planning the menu and purchasing the food and made sure that none of our ingredients had been produced in factories that use peanuts in their products.

"Then Detective Goldman went through the list of guests and our relationship to them." She took another sip of the tea. "He even asked about you and Zachary. What did he think? That you poisoned Melvin? Fed him peanuts? Hah. I told him he was barking up the wrong tree."

Where did the idea of poison come from? Surely not from Goldman. That word, spoken so casually in relation to Mr.

Schwartz's death, made the hair on my arms stand at attention. If the autopsy results indicated that the cause of death was poison or even the result of his allergy, *A Fine Fix* would forever be linked and our reputation washed down the drain.

A silence hovered around us, heavy as the humidity in the air. A crow squawked across the patio and alighted on a tree limb.

Zach paled as he and Ally exchanged a glance. "Are you staying with your mom?" he asked her.

He'd been so quiet, I was surprised he'd decided to join the living. His intense gaze toward Ally seemed to have some significance.

"For a while," she answered. I couldn't see her eyes behind the dark glasses, but I sensed the same intensity in her voice. "We need each other for support."

"What do you think happened to your dad?" I blurted, without thinking. A bead of sweat slid down my back. In the burgundy polyester suit I'd worn to my appointment with Barbara Lewis, I roasted like a chicken in the oven, needing to be basted. I gulped my iced tea and held the cool, sweaty glass to my cheek and neck.

Ally glanced at Zach then lifted her chin. "I don't have a clue what happened to Daddy."

I could smell something going on between these two as if a flounder fillet had been left out in the hot sun.


"OKAY, ZACH," I said on the drive home. "Fess up. Something's going on between you and Ally, and I want to know what it is. Now." I'd had enough of Zach's evasiveness. As long as I'd known him, there had never been any secrets between us. At least that's what I thought.

"Nothing's going on," he said, staring out the car window.

"That's a bunch of crab! Come on, I know you like I know the blade of my Santoku."

Zach knew I didn't use obscenities, but he also knew that when I came close, I meant business.

He leaned back on the headrest, closed his eyes and sighed. "I've got this...thing for Allison."

"Tell me something I don't know."

He hung his head. "Since the first time I met her. When I visited you at school. Remember?"

"You visited me lots of times. I don't remember the first time."

"Freshman year. You were in class." His voice was quiet. "I missed you, Trudie. So I went to your dorm room to surprise you. I hadn't told you I was coming."

I nodded. "I know. I missed you, too."

"But that day," he continued, "I walked into your room, and there she was, sitting cross-legged on her bed, studying."

"Oh, yeah. Was that Homecoming Weekend? I think I do remember."

"Yes. That's it." His voice became animated. "Anyway, there was this angel sitting on the bed. She just gazed up at me with those innocent blue eyes and asked if she could help me. I tell you, Trudie, I wanted to dive into those eyes."

Uh-oh, I thought. I knew exactly what he was talking about. I was her roommate. Every guy who ever met Ally reacted the same way.

"Heck, Zach. You're a man. You were attracted to her. That's normal."

He frowned, his eyes darkening. "No. How I felt that day, and every day since, is not normal. It's—it's…" He searched for the right word. "…an obsession." He put his hand over his eyes and hung his head.

We were stopped at a light, so I pulled his hand down. "Zach, look at me. It's okay to have strong feelings for someone and not have those feelings returned. We move on as best we can." God knows, I've had my share of unrequited love.

He faced me, but his eyes were focused somewhere else. "That first weekend, she asked me to take her to some sorority party. It was one of those uptight sororities, and Allison wanted to make a good impression, didn't want to bring a jock or a frat boy who would get drunk and embarrass her."

"I remember that. You did her a big favor. It was sweet of you." The light changed to green, and I stepped on the gas.

"So we went to the party, but she started drinking and drinking, heavily, and ended up embarrassing herself. I made excuses that she was sick, got her out of there and was driving her back to the dorm." He shook his head and pounded his fist on the dashboard.

This was a side of Zach I'd never seen before. "Go on," I urged, keeping my eyes on the road.

"Ally was upset that she'd messed up and wouldn't get a bid from the sorority. She started crying and made me pull the car over.

Trudie, all I tried to do was comfort her. I put my arm around her and held her. Then she started kissing me and telling me to make love to her. She was unbuttoning my shirt and my pants, taking off her clothes." He opened his mouth to continue, but just shook his head.

Zach and Ally? I'd suspected that something had happened between them, but never thought it had gone that far. I tried to wrap my mind around all of this as if I were preparing an egg roll, trying to keep the filling from coming out.

He found his voice. "I…I tried to pull a condom out of my wallet, but she wouldn't wait. She kept begging me to do it already, and climbed on top of me." He shook his head. "I couldn't hold back. Oh god, Trudie, she was drunk, and I just went ahead and took advantage of her."

I paused to take all this in. He wouldn't be the first guy to do a thing like that. Only someone like Zach would still feel guilty after all these years. How many guys even remember conquests from their younger days, much less feel bad about them?

Zach must have taken my silence as some sort of rebuke. "Look," he spouted. "I'm only human, you know. I was only giving her what she wanted. It might have happened even if she hadn't gotten drunk. It was pretty obvious I wasn't her first."

"No, she wasn't a virgin." I remembered many late nights at school when Ally had stumbled into the dorm room giggling, her clothes jumbled.

"When Allison came home for Thanksgiving, she called me." His voice was quieter now. "She was pregnant."

"Pregnant?"

I swerved the car over to the curb and jammed on the brakes.

"Jesus, Trudie. Are you trying to kill us? It's a good thing we have our seat belts on." He turned to me, wide-eyed.

"If I wanted to kill you, I would have done it long ago. Right now, tell me about this pregnancy."

"She was upset. Said she wasn't like her birth mother and wasn't going to give her baby away like it was some old sweater she couldn't use. I didn't even know she was adopted. She wanted me to go with her to the abortion clinic." Zach ran his fingers through his hair. "I tried to talk her out of it, told her I would marry her, if she wanted. But she didn't want that. I suggested adoption. She wouldn't hear any of it. So, I went with her and it was done."

Thoughts sloshed around in my head like milk in a coconut. Something this important and Zach never confided in me? Did he think it would ruin our friendship? After all these years, it hurt that he didn't trust me enough to tell me. Ally was my roommate, but we were never that close. Even so, why did she have to mess with my best friend?

I understood Ally's attraction and her influence over men. In this instance, she had taken advantage of Zach, not the other way around. But she was drunk. He could have refused, no matter how hard, no pun intended. I just couldn't escape the fact that she was pregnant and Zach, even though he said he tried to change her mind, had helped her get an abortion.

Watching him, submerged in his guilt and regret, tears came to my eyes. "Oh, Zach." I reached over and squeezed his hand. Ally surely must have suffered because of her decision to terminate the pregnancy. But it was Zach, and what he had gone through, that I cried for now. Thinking back about Ally's wild jaunts at school, I wondered if it had really been Zach's baby.

"There are other things you don't know." His Adam's apple moved as he swallowed. His fist clenched beneath mine.

"Ever since then, Ally has this hold over me. She asks me to do things for her, and I always do them."

With this revelation, I jerked my head up to Zach. My body began to tremble, and the hairs on my arms stood up. "Zach?"

He turned to face me.

"Did Ally have something to do with her father's death?"

Zach's eyebrows drew together, and he looked me squarely in the eyes. He shook his head. "I honestly don't know."

# Chapter Seven

We sat on the floor in Zach's living room eating a margherita pizza. He and I had a lot of serious talking to do, but we'd been out all afternoon, it was almost seven o'clock, and I was hungry. I think better on a full stomach. I was on my third piece, while Zach had barely finished his first.

"So let's go over this again. Ally made some kind of treat for her father and asked you to give it to him at the party?"

Zach shook his head. "Well, not exactly. Graciella handed me a plastic container she'd found on the foyer table. Taped to the top was an envelope with my name on it."

"And—"

"And there was a note to me from Ally saying she was late for a dinner date but had made these treats for her father because she'd missed his birthday last week. She asked me to make sure he got them." Zach picked pieces of tomato and basil off his pizza and popped them into his mouth.

"What kind of treats? Ally doesn't even like to cook. Why would she make something for her father, especially knowing that we would be catering his party?"

"Cookie bars. The kind you bake with graham crackers and chocolate chips and coconut. Evidently, they're his favorites. To tell you the truth, I tried one myself. It was delicious."

"Wait a minute." I put my paper plate on the coffee table and rose to my knees. "Peanuts. Were there any peanuts in this concoction?"

"I—I don't recall. I don't think so."

"Zach, we both know Mr. Schwartz had a peanut allergy. When we went over the menu with Mrs. Schwartz, she said, 'Absolutely no peanuts. My husband is deathly allergic.' His own daughter would know that, wouldn't she?"

"Trudie, what are you implying? That she purposely made something that would hurt her father? Well I'm not buying it. Sure, Ally has her faults. She's vain, she's irresponsible with money, she's promiscuous, self-centered, divisive." He counted them off on his fingers. "And if I thought about it, I could probably come up with several more. But she would never do anything to hurt her father."

"Zach, you weren't so sure when we were sitting in the car earlier."

"I was freaked out. But Ally loved her father. She wouldn't give him anything with peanuts."

"Hold on." I closed my eyes and tried to visualize a plastic container sitting at the bar next to Zach, or even Zach delivering them to the intended party. Nothing came to mind. "What happened to the treats? Did you give them to Mr. Schwartz?"

Zach frowned. "Actually, I didn't. Every time I spotted him, someone was giving me a drink order. I figured I'd deliver them later when there was more time. So I set the container on the bar next to me. A few of the guests sampled them while they waited for their drinks."

I nodded. This all sounded plausible, as I had only spotted Mr. Schwartz one time that evening speaking with Mr. and Mrs. Lewis.

"Wait a minute. I remember." Zach stood up and started pacing. "I couldn't leave the bar so I asked one of the guests. He said that he'd seen Mr. Schwartz by the cabana and would be glad to bring the cookie bars down to him."

"Which guest was it?" I asked, getting to my feet. "Who was it? Did he actually give them to Mr. Schwartz?"

"I don't know. I was busy making drinks." Zach sank onto the couch like a deflated balloon.

"What did he look like? What was he wearing?"

"They were all wearing polo shirts and chinos." He shook his head. "Even if all the male guests stood in a line-up, I'm not sure I could tell you which one it was."

"I don't know. I don't know. That's all I hear from you. Think, Zach. Think. You have to be more observant when you're working a party. Especially when you're working the bar."

"Like your friend Bradley, the bartender?" he scowled. "I guess I need to be more like the whiz kid—Mr. Personality, Mr. Dishwasher, Mr. Wine Finder, Mr. Dimple Smile. Face it. Even Barbara Lewis requested him over me."

For a moment, we stared at each other in silence.

I hadn't meant to hurt his feelings. I sat down next to him on the sofa and put my head on his shoulder. When he turned to me, I glanced up.

"You know what, Zach? There isn't anyone who can prep a meal like you or serve like you or leave a kitchen as spotless as you can. We're a team, and no one can replace you, ever."

I tilted my head up to him. We were almost nose to nose. He studied me as if seeing me for the first time, took my face in his hands and kissed me. It was a gentle kiss, soft and warm, and his lips tasted of oregano and basil. I leaned in to his kiss, and his hands slid behind my back and pulled me closer.

I closed my eyes to savor the moment.

No. I pulled back and leapt to my feet like a Mexican jumping bean. "Zach! Oh my god, what are we doing?" I fled across the room and stood on the other side of the coffee table.

"What's wrong?" he asked. "I thought you enjoyed it."

"I did. I mean, I didn't. I mean…." I didn't know what I meant, but I had to put a stop to this right now. He and I were best friends and business partners and that's all we were. "Let's not complicate things, Zach."

"But Trudie, that was nice, wasn't it?"

The huge grin on his face caused me to smile. It was good to see him snap out of his gloomy mood.

"Yes. I have to admit, it was nice. But we have a business to run. Let's wait until things calm down. Then we can talk. Right now," I said, checking my watch, "we've got a contract to write for Barbara Lewis."

"Okay." He smiled. "When things calm down, we'll talk."

ABOUT TEN, I finally arrived home. The first thing I do when I get home, after throwing my purse onto the sofa, is walk straight to the kitchen. Or to be more specific, the refrigerator. Okay, so I had just eaten six out of the eight slices of pizza. Zach didn't have much of an appetite. But that was almost three hours ago. A girl gets hungry.

Opening the door of the fridge, I cringed. With everything that had happened, I'd forgotten all about the cabbage soup diet I'd been on all week. Containers of cabbage soup filled the shelves. I'd read about the diet in *Good Housekeeping* magazine, which showed several before and after shots of people who'd lost tons of weight.

I pulled out a container and opened the lid. "Blech," I gagged. After five days on this stuff, I should have lost ten pounds. I slid the scale out of the corner. I had read somewhere that keeping a scale in the kitchen is a deterrent to bingeing. So far, it hadn't worked for me, but I didn't see any reason to move it back into the bathroom.

Setting the soup on the counter, I slipped off my shoes, stepped onto the scale and waited for the digital display to register a number. I'd gained three pounds. Three pounds. Turning back to the refrigerator, I removed all the containers of soup, pulled off their lids and dumped every one of them into the sink. I flipped on the switch and fed the whole mess to the garbage disposal, enjoying the grinding and gurgling sounds as it swallowed up the cabbage soup.

As I washed out the containers, I thought of all the dishes Bradley and I had cleaned the night before. Bradley. I'd forgotten to call him about working the Lewis party Saturday night. I retrieved my catering apron hanging on a hook in the bedroom and found the business card with his phone number. Hanging alongside my apron was the one Bradley had worn. I'd brought them both home to wash. I pulled the card out of my apron pocket. In a bold block print, his note said, "Call me anytime. I'm up late. Bradley."

I glanced at the clock. It was late, but I picked up the receiver and punched in his number. The scent of his cologne had lingered on the apron, hinting of spice and citrus. I held it up to my nose and inhaled. I could still feel his arm around me as he'd tried to calm me down last night.

He answered after the first ring. "Trudie, it's great to hear from you so soon."

I paused, wondering how he knew it was me.

"Caller ID," he said, reading my mind.

Hearing his voice again, my heart started to flutter.

"Hi, Bradley. Hope it's not too late to call." I hugged the apron.

"It's never too late. I'm a night owl. Most of my jobs are at night, and—"

"And what?" I prompted.

"I—used to stay up with Mom waiting for my dad to get home. But enough about that. What can I do for you?"

"I have a dinner party booked for Saturday night. They specifically asked for you. Are you available?"

"Asked for me? Who are they?"

"Guests at the party last night. They're the people you retrieved the bottle of wine for."

"Oh yeah, the Lewises. I remember them. Barbara and Robert, right?"

"Exactly. You have an amazing memory." I thought about Zach and how he couldn't recall what any of the guests even looked like. Bradley not only remembered them, he knew their names.

"Hard to forget. Mrs. Lewis pretended to lose her footing on the stone patio and held onto my arm for support. Then she wouldn't let go. Happens all the time."

He didn't sound conceited or egotistic, just nonchalant and resigned to the facts of his life.

"Well, are you?" I asked.

"Am I what?"

"Available, to work the Lewis party."

"Yes, and I'd be happy to work with you again, Trudie."

"Great. I'll call you back with the details later in the week. Thanks, Bradley."

When I hung up, my insides danced with anticipation like the tiny bubbles in sparkling wine.

I'd had these feelings once, in high school, when I was assigned to tutor Greg Ballard in Algebra. Greg was popular, very cute, always had a girlfriend, and never noticed me. But in our tutoring sessions, he was attentive and nice. He talked to me as if I were a good friend. Every time I went to meet him, I pretended I was going on a date to meet my secret lover. In the halls at school, he wouldn't stop to talk. I knew he thought it would damage his reputation. But he'd always give me a quick wink, like we had something together, just the two of us. The relationship, such as it was, ended with the semester when he aced his Algebra exam. I never forgot that feeling of excited anticipation before each meeting.

I held the apron to my nose again and inhaled. Last night, Bradley and I had connected, in a weird sense because of similar but opposite experiences growing up. We understood each other, and if nothing else, we might become friends.

Then I remembered that kiss with Zach. After such a long, close friendship with him, I'd never even considered him in romantic terms. We were as close as any two people could be. And we truly loved each other. But not in that way.

His kiss felt good. Natural. I hadn't wanted it to end.

So why did I break away from him? Of course, I knew the answer. A relationship like that would ruin our bond of friendship and the rapport we'd had all these years cooking together. Working side by side with Zach provided the comfort and security I needed to make our business thrive. I couldn't let that change.

I wondered if the kiss had merely been a way to release the stress of all that had happened over the last twenty-four hours. As I told Zach, we needed to wait for things to calm down and life to go back to normal. Then we could evaluate our feelings for each other.

My stomach growled. For now, I was hungry.

I went back into the kitchen, pulled out my biggest frying pan and retrieved a package of bacon from the freezer. Prying off six strips, I dropped them one by one into the pan. When they were brown and sizzling, I cracked in three eggs to cook in the grease. The heck with cabbage soup. Tonight, I would begin a low-carb diet.

# Chapter Eight

Every time I pull up to the entrance of *A Fine Fix*, my heart feels like a sweet potato swelling in the oven. I am a business owner.

Just a small warehouse off Nebel Street in Rockville, my shop sits amidst a row of others, a printing and mailing service, a plumbing supply house, a flooring and carpeting showroom and an auto upholstery shop. My neighbors and I have an understanding. We help each other out, patronize each other's business. Janine next door designed and printed my business cards at a discount and Jake installed a new headliner in my Honda when the fabric kept drooping down on my head. And when Manny held a special one-day flooring event and open house, *A Fine Fix* provided the punch and pastries at no charge.

On Monday morning, Zach's VW bug sat out front, and the company van was backed up to the loading dock. I pushed open the customer entrance door with our logo etched into the glass. The décor of our office reflects who we are—quirky but chic. Manny, our flooring neighbor, had scanned dozens of catalogs until he'd found the perfect purple carpeting with orange swirls. I'd located a fabulous birch desk at the used furniture store in our office park, and we'd hung oversized art deco posters on the walls. An antique white distressed table and chairs provided an area where clients could select table settings and view sample menus in a comfortable and welcoming atmosphere.

"Good morning, Zach," I shouted. He wasn't in the office, so I knew he must be busy in the warehouse, where we store all our equipment: pots, pans, china, glassware, silverware, linens. The warehouse is also where we keep our pride and joy, a twelve-foot by eight-foot walk-in—a room-sized, aluminum refrigerator with a freezer in the back—a treasure we'd purchased used when a restaurant up the street went out of business.

"Be there in a minute," he yelled from the back. He was probably reshelving the supplies from the Schwartz party. I'm sure this was the first chance he'd had with all that had occurred over the last couple of days.

I sat at the desk and tried to settle my nerves, wiping my moist palms on the sides of my turquoise sherbet capris. In all the years I'd known Zach, I had never been apprehensive about seeing him. Why in the world did he have to kiss me and change everything?

"Hi." His voice startled me. Then I saw his sheepish grin, hands sunk in his pants pockets. Was he nervous, too?

I noticed that his normally curly hair was flat on one side as if he'd slept on it all night. "Don't you ever look in a mirror?" I walked over to him and held out my hand, palm up. "Comb."

He pulled a pick comb out of his back pocket and handed it to me.

I stood on tiptoe and reached up to correct the damage, using the pick to pull out his natural curls. Zach dipped his head down to me, holding my gaze for a moment. I could feel the warmth of his breath. "There. Not perfect, but better."

After so many years of working side-by-side with Zach, why did this closeness feel so awkward? I handed him his comb and stood back. "Remember, we have to deliver the contract to Barbara Lewis today and should at least be presentable."

"Yeah, I know. See, I wore khakis today instead of jeans. And a white polo. Very clean cut, wouldn't you say?"

"It'll do." I walked back to the desk and turned on the PC. I didn't want to lead him on, just wanted to forget about what had happened last night and get to work.

"It'll do? Isn't this exactly what your all-American model, Bradley Miller, would wear?"

"What is this obsession you have about Bradley?" I couldn't understand what he had against Bradley, who had only been sweet and supportive to me. In fact, Zach had to be the only person who didn't like Bradley.

"Obsession? I don't think I'm the one with the obsession."

"Zach, I don't know what your problem is, but get over it already. We've got work to do. Now where did you put the contract details we worked on last night? I want to enter them into the computer and print it out. I told Mrs. Lewis we'd be there about eleven."

"Sorry. They're right here." He pulled up a chair and pointed to a folder that was sitting on the desk. "Trudie, can I just say one more thing first?"

"All right," I sighed. "Go ahead."

He covered my hand with his. "We've been friends as long as I can remember and will remain friends forever, no matter what." He gazed into my eyes. "Right?"

I nodded.

"So even though I said some things last night and even though I kissed you, I want you to know that nothing has changed. Nothing. We are still BFF."

"BFF?"

"Best Friends Forever. You know. It's cell phone text lingo. I'm not very fast with those little keys, so I'm trying to learn some short cuts. What I'm not so sure of, though, is whether LOL is Lots of Luck or Laughing Out Loud."

We both broke out laughing.

"So BFF?" He held out his pinky.

"BFF." I said, hooking my pinky around his and feeling my whole body relax. No one knew how to make me feel better than Zach did. Smiling, I opened the folder and got to work.

THIS TIME, I found a parking space right across the street from the Lewis house. When the maid let us in, we assumed we knew the drill and headed for the drawing room.

"This way, Miss Fine," she called from behind us. When we turned, her arm was extended to the opposite side of the foyer. She cleared her throat. "Mrs. Lewis would like to see you in the library today."

"Oh." I made an about-face, straightened my turquoise jacket and adjusted the matching headband as she drew back the French doors.

Zach and I walked slowly into an enormous hunter green room with massive mahogany built-in bookcases and the smell of rich leather. I felt as if we were about to meet the Wizard of Oz. Rising from her throne-like chair behind the desk, Barbara Lewis, in fact, was wearing an emerald green dress.

"Ms. Fine." She smiled. "And Mr.—"

"Cohen," Zach said.

"Yes, Mr. Cohen. So nice to see you again." She sat down, gesturing for us to sit in the two Queen Anne chairs that faced the desk.

After reviewing the menu and discussing the terms of the contract, Barbara Lewis wrote out and signed her deposit check in majestic scrolling letters. When she placed the check in a pale blue parchment envelope, I almost expected her to stamp it with a royal wax seal. She smiled and stood to hand it to me as a gesture of dismissal.

"Uh, Mrs. Lewis," I ventured, taking the envelope. "Would you mind giving me just another moment? Could I ask you some questions about the party the other night? I'm curious about a few things." It bothered me that Goldman seemed to be focusing his entire investigation on Zach and overlooking everyone else who'd been at that party. Barbara Lewis and her husband had spoken to Mr. Schwartz before he died. They had also spoken to Bradley. Maybe they had seen or heard something without realizing it.

Her smile faded. "I have a very busy schedule, Miss Fine."

"I'm sure you do, Mrs. Lewis. It's just that…you see…Mr. Schwartz was a friend. Well, the father of my friend, Allison. I just thought…maybe the police have missed something, some small detail that will shed light on how Mr. Schwartz died." I wondered if she could hear the trembling in my voice. This woman was beyond intimidating, and I hoped she wouldn't cancel our contract completely and demand that I return the check.

"And you think that I might be the person who can provide that small detail." Barbara Lewis' posture was stiff as she stood behind the desk.

"I don't know. You may have seen something, or heard something, that seemed innocent at the time."

Slowly she lowered herself back into her chair. "All right. What would you like to know?"

I sat down and crossed my legs. "You mentioned that Mr. Schwartz wanted you to try a special wine that night. How long did you speak with him?"

"Let me think. Robert, that is Mr. Lewis, had already been speaking with Melvin for a time. They were having words, and I wanted to step in to change the tone of their conversation. I mentioned that the margaritas were wonderful, but I wondered if there was a wine that would pair nicely with Mexican food."

"And that's when he sent Brad—I mean the bartender—to the wine cellar," Zach prompted.

"Yes. That is correct. Lovely young man."

Zach gave me a glance that said, "See, everyone likes Bradley better."

I turned back to Barbara Lewis. "And did you continue to talk with Mr. Schwartz after that?"

She shook her head. "Oh no. Melvin excused himself to speak to other guests. Then Robert and I sampled your marvelous hors d'oeuvres. We can't wait to serve your food to our guests on Saturday night."

"Thank you. I'm so glad you got a chance to taste some things." I was proud of our food. We worked hard to make every dish unique and delicious, and a compliment from someone who probably dines at the finest restaurants meant a lot to me.

I saw her glance at her watch, definitely a signal meant for us.

"Just one more question, Mrs. Lewis." I leaned forward. "What do you think Mr. Schwartz and your husband were discussing so seriously?"

She sat up straighter. "Well, if I could take a guess, it was probably business-related. They had dealings. Buildings. Real estate. That sort of thing." She waved her hand through the air as if whisking away those pesky subjects, then stood. "Thank you for being so prompt with the contract. Good day."

Duly dismissed, Zach and I left.

"Zach, did you hear Mr. Schwartz and Mr. Lewis 'having words,' as she described it, at the party?" I asked after we'd gotten into the car.

"When she mentioned that, I did remember Mr. Schwartz getting into it a little with some guy. Their voices were raised, and Mr. Schwartz's face was red."

"And then what happened?"

Zach squinted out the front windshield as if trying to picture the scene. "Nothing after that. A couple of guests came over to the bar and gave me their orders." He turned to me. "That must have been about the time Barbara Lewis interrupted them to defuse the argument."

"And probably about the time that Bradley arrived," I added, giving Zach a meaningful smile.

He just rolled his eyes at me and shook his head. "Let's go."


THAT AFTERNOON I was back at my desk working up the Lewis party shopping list when the door jingled someone's arrival. "Please, have a seat," I said, focusing on the computer screen. "I'll be with you in a moment." I clicked the save icon and glanced up.

Detective Goldman was surveying the room.

I inhaled a big gulp of air. What was he doing here? "And to what do I owe this pleasure?" I hoped he heard the sarcasm in my voice.

"Just in the neighborhood and thought I'd drop in to say hello. Nice place you have here." He'd had that same mocking smirk the last time I'd seen him at the police station.

"You know, some of us have work to do," I said.

"I'm working, too. Just wanted to ask a few questions. Can you take a break?" He appeared to be wearing the same wrinkled jacket and pants from Saturday night.

"How long of a break?" Zach was doing some errands for me, and I was afraid he'd be back soon. He might freak out if he saw Goldman's car parked outside.

"Have you had lunch?"

Had lunch? I was starving. That was the main reason Zach had gone out—to pick up grilled chicken salads at the deli around the corner. "Not yet."

"Me neither," he said. "Why don't we go up the road to the Silver Diner? I don't make it out to the 'burbs too often, and we don't have anything like it in the District."

He wanted to have lunch with me? Why? If he had more questions about Saturday night, I didn't have much to tell. I'd already told him everything I knew, which wasn't much since I'd been in the Schwartz's kitchen cooking all afternoon and evening. Anything else he wanted to know he could ask here, right now.

"I'll give you one hour and that's it." I scribbled a note to Zach, "Couldn't wait. Remembered something I had to do." I felt bad bailing on him when he'd offered to get us lunch, but more importantly, I wanted to get the detective out of here before Zach returned.

The thought that Goldman might actually want to have lunch with me made my stomach feel like a pot of water about to reach the boiling point, little bubbles forming around the edges. Like hope bubbling up inside that someone would actually be interested in me, Trudie Fine. Not that the detective was someone I'd be interested in, with his snide remarks.

SITTING IN A booth across from Daniel Goldman, I flipped through the songs on the mini jukebox attached to the wall. He'd ordered a burger, fries and a black and white milkshake, while I had asked for a bunless burger with coleslaw and a diet coke. I was determined to stick to my low-carb plan. "Got a quarter?" I asked.

He reached into his pocket and tossed a coin to me. Fumbling to catch it, I plucked it from my cleavage before it could take the fatal plunge. I felt my face redden and was not surprised to see the detective grinning at me. He'd probably intended that as the target all along.

I turned away, inserted the coin into the jukebox and pressed A12, *Love Me Tender.* All the songs were from the fifties and sixties, and I was a sucker for Elvis with that deep, mellow voice, vibrating through my body. "By the time the song comes on, we'll probably be gone," I said. "But I'll risk it."

"Hey, that's my quarter you're risking." He nodded toward the jukebox.

"If they don't play it, I'll owe you. So, Detective, how is the investigation going? Do you know how Mr. Schwartz died yet?"

"Too soon to tell." He stared at me with those intense eyes just like the other night in the Schwartzes' living room.

I looked down and ran my finger along the creamy swirled pattern on the Formica table. "What about the autopsy?" I asked, peering back at him. "Have they done it yet? I know Mrs. Schwartz and Ally were both very anxious about that."

"The ME is performing the autopsy today. Of course, it will take a couple days to get lab results, pathology reports, that kind of thing."

"Finally," I said, relieved. "At least we'll know how the poor man died. That should close the case. Right?"

"Should," he nodded. Getting information from him was like trying to squeeze juice from an unpeeled pineapple.

"You wanted to ask me some questions?" Supposedly, that was the reason he'd asked me to lunch. Of course, now I did have new information—the cookie bars Ally had made for her father. Just an innocent piece of information but one that could incriminate Zach, and I wasn't going to be the one to tell the detective about it. "Remember, you only have an hour."

"You have to eat, don't you? We've got time." He took out his notepad and pen.

"So this is part of your official investigation, I see." The bubbling inside me deflated as I realized Detective Goldman's true intention for having lunch with me. Not that I was interested in him, but the reality of the situation did hurt my pride. Just another guy pretending to like me for his own purposes.

"I want to get everything down correctly. Don't worry. I'll put this away when the food comes. So, Miss Fine. May I call you Trudie?"

"I guess." I certainly didn't want to be called Miss Fine.

"Trudie, how long have you known Zachary Cohen?"

"What? You're back on that kick about Zach? What kind of detective are you? Zach is the kindest, most harmless person I know. For you to accuse him of something is...is..." I could feel my blood pressure rising.

"Trudie, I'm not accusing Zach of anything. I'm just asking you some questions. I'm trying to eliminate him as a person of interest. That's all. And you can help with that."

"A person of interest? That's the same thing as a suspect. I cannot, for the life of me, understand why you keep focusing on him. If you think there was some kind of foul play, shouldn't you be out there pursuing the real person of interest?" I was losing my appetite, an unfamiliar sensation.

His voice became very quiet. "Trudie, just let me ask you a few questions. You know Zach better than anyone, don't you? He's your partner, right?"

I nodded.

"Then let's get this over and done with, check his name off and move on to someone else. Okay?" His voice was almost soothing.

"Okay." I released a deep sigh. "I've known Zach since we were kids, maybe six years old."

"You've remained friends all these years?" His face was serious now, but there was a definite glimmer in his eyes. Hazel eyes, I noticed for the first time.

"Yes." What kind of interrogation was this?

"Ever gone beyond friendship?" There was that smirk again.

"What?" My voice was pitched higher than a tuning fork. "How dare you ask me that? Fudge you, Detective Goldman." I grabbed my purse, slid from the booth, and turned to leave.

I could walk back to the office. It wasn't that far.

Aretha Franklin's voice sang out in the background, *R-E-S-P-E-C-T, find out what it means to me...oh, a little respect, yeah, baby, I want a little respect...*

"Trudie, wait." His hand grazed my shoulder.

I swung around. "Wait for what? For you to harass me some more? Every time I agree to cooperate, I feel as if you're pouring hot gravy over my head."

*All I want, ooh yeah, I want a little respect.*

He took a step back, his hands up as if to shield himself from my onslaught.

The waiter arrived with our lunches and placed them on our table. He looked back and forth between us. "Are you leaving?"

People in adjacent booths were watching us, too.

Goldman gazed down at me. "I have a confession to make. I lied to you."

"About what?" I peered at our uneaten food on the table. My stomach growled. I could hear it above Aretha's voice.

"Sit down and I'll tell you. Please." He gestured to our booth.

We returned to the table.

"Go ahead. I'm waiting."

He picked up his straw and thumped it on the table until it poked through the paper at the top. "I led you to believe this lunch was all about getting information. That wasn't my real purpose."

"It wasn't? Then why…?"

"I wanted to see you again. And I didn't think you'd go to lunch with me if I asked." He tied the white paper around the top of the straw.

"It would have been a heck of a lot easier if you'd just asked."

"Would you have said yes?"

"Try me." I squeezed ketchup onto my burger and layered the lettuce and tomato slice on top.

"Trudie, will you have lunch with me today?"

"Absolutely not, Detective Goldman," I said, cutting into my burger and placing that first juicy morsel into my mouth. "But I can't let this food go to waste."

"Daniel. Call me Daniel." His bangs had fallen over his forehead, and I noticed his eyes were more bronze than hazel. When I'd first met him Saturday night, I thought he might have been about forty. His eyes drooped a little at the corners, giving him a weary look. I guessed a job like this takes its toll on a person. Now I realized he was probably younger, maybe thirty-four or thirty-five.

"Daniel," I said.

He waved the straw like a flag, the white paper dragging through the air. "Truce?"

I smiled. I guess my intuition had been correct after all. He was interested in me.

The music changed, and Elvis poured his heart out from the speakers. *Love me tender, love me sweet, never let me go….*

# Chapter Nine

"**G**ood afternoon, *A Fine Fix*," I answered in my most professional voice. It was almost five o'clock. I had already powered down the computer and was anxious to get home, change into something comfortable and grill myself a thick, juicy steak. Why do people insist on calling at the end of the day?

"Trudie?"

"Ally?" I knew the voice right away. After all, we'd been roommates for four years at Johnson and Wales. But I don't remember her ever calling me at work and wondered what she wanted, or needed, from me. "Is your mom okay?" I hadn't called Mrs. Schwartz today to check on her.

"Yes, she's fine—considering we're still waiting for the autopsy results."

"Is something wrong?"

She hesitated. "I need to talk to you if you have a few minutes."

"Sure," I said. "I'm listening." I wished she would get to the point already. I'd found a new steak seasoning at the Penzeys Spices store on Rockville Pike and was dying to try it. My mouth watered at the thought.

"Not now. I mean, not on the phone. I need to speak to you in private. Can you meet me?"

"Meet you now? Where?" Allison lived in a condo on Connecticut Avenue in northwest D.C. At this time of day, in rush hour traffic and with all those stop lights, it would take me forever to get there. "I have plans." She didn't have to know that I had an appointment with a twelve-ounce rib eye.

"Please, Trudie. I really need to see you today. I promise not to keep you long. We can meet half way. There's a wine bar in Chevy Chase, on Wisconsin Avenue. Free hors d'oeuvres until six-thirty." Ally knew my weaknesses.

"Okay. I'll give you half an hour. Then I'll have to go."

"Great. And, uh, Trudie, please don't tell Zach you're meeting me. Okay?"

I glanced up. Zach had just come in from the warehouse to prepare the display area for the prospective client we'd be meeting with in the morning. He glanced at me, his eyebrows raised in a questioning manner, silently asking who was on the phone. I felt my face color. I wasn't used to keeping things from him. In fact, until the Schwartz party, my life and my comings and goings had been an open book to Zach. In the past few days, however, I'd been forced by circumstances to keep secrets from him, and I didn't like it one bit. I hoped that my abrupt wave of a hand and shake of my head would signal him that this call was nothing worth sharing.

Still, I worried about why Ally would want our meeting kept from Zach. Was she going to share their relationship with me? Or did this have something to do with her father's death? Some information she had? A confession?

"Who are you giving only half an hour?" Zach asked when I'd hung up.

"Just a new seafood vendor. Said he'd come by sometime next week." I avoided eye contact with him, neatly stacking the folders on my desk and retrieving my purse from the bottom file drawer. One look into my face and he'd know I was lying. "See you tomorrow," I called over my shoulder as I walked out the door.

ENTERING THE DARKENED bar, I stood for a moment waiting for my eyes to adjust. Several people sitting at the bar turned to inspect me. In my turquoise outfit, I must have resembled a rainbow-sprinkled birthday cupcake amidst a sea of decadent chocolate mousse desserts.

I spotted Ally in a dark booth at the back corner of the restaurant. When I reached her table, she stood to give me a quick peck on each cheek. Her blonde hair spilled over the shoulders of a short, black sleeveless sheath.

I had always envied women who could effortlessly slip into a dress and heels and look gorgeous. For me, getting dressed involved several attempts and a bed covered in garments that were too tight to button or that exposed flabby arms that resembled legs of lamb.

I slid into the semi-circular booth next to Ally, and the waiter placed a glass of cabernet and a plate of wings in front of me.

I glanced at him and then at Ally.

"I took the liberty of ordering your wine to save time," she said. "The wings are complimentary."

Her serious demeanor prompted me to get down to business. "So what's up?"

She waited until the server walked away and then bent her head toward me. "I think I may be in trouble," she whispered.

Was she pregnant again? By the dark expression in her eyes, I realized it was something else. Anyway, she'd never told me about the first baby. Why would she tell me about another? "What kind of trouble?"

"That pesky Detective Goldman keeps questioning me."

"You, too?" It surprised me. I thought Zach was the only one he'd been bombarding. I also felt a tinge of jealousy. Had he been bugging Ally just so he could spend time with her, too? Did he use his job as a ploy to be with women? Certainly Ally was a lot more desirable than I was.

"He's been interrogating you?" Her blue eyes were wide.

"Not me. Zach. But what is he questioning you about? You weren't even at the party."

She took a sip of her chardonnay, sighed and gazed down at her lap. "He suspects it was something Daddy ate that caused his death. He knows that I baked cookie bars and asked Zach to deliver them to Daddy." She faced me and took hold of my arm. "Trudie, I knew

Daddy was deathly allergic to peanuts. I would never knowingly put peanuts in the ingredients. Do you believe me?"

Her expression was guileless and open. "Yes, of course I believe you." And now that I was with Ally, I did believe her. When we were at school, she talked to her father almost every day on the phone, and she spoke about him all the time—Daddy did this and Daddy said that. He was her hero, and she loved him. "But what difference does it make what I think?"

She sat up straighter. "Because Goldman's going to ask you about me, and you know me best. Trudie, you can vouch for me, and he'll believe you."

I turned to sip my wine and feeling a rumbling in my stomach, plucked a chicken wing from the plate and took a bite. Hmm. Nice recipe, just the right amount of spicy heat. The skin could be crispier, though.

"Trudie, would you vouch for me?" she persisted.

"Let me ask you a question." I wiped my mouth and fingers with the white cloth napkin, for a second wondering what laundry service the bar used, with all the barbeque sauce and red wine smears that must stain their linens. "Why did you tell me not to mention our meeting to Zach?"

Her eyes shifted to the right, and I remembered seeing on a detective show that this gesture indicated the person was hiding something or lying.

"Zach and I have a past, and he knows some things about me."

"Like what?" He'd told me about the pregnancy and abortion, but what else was there to tell?

"We dated on and off," she ran her fingers up and down the stem of the wine glass.

"And?"

"And there was some trouble."

"When?" Okay, now she was going to tell about the pregnancy and abortion.

She inhaled and emitted a small, high-pitched sob. "Back in college. I visited Zach at UM. He'd asked me to the Homecoming game and a dance his dorm was having."

"Okay," I said. "So you and Zach went out. Then what?"

"Some people were bringing food to the party, so Zach and I decided to make these dessert bars. It was kind of fun cooking with him." She smiled.

"I know," I said, feeling a little jealous again, thinking about that kiss last night. "I cook with him every day. He's a great partner."

"We put everything in those bars but the kitchen sink—chocolate chips, oatmeal, marshmallows, coconut, caramels." Her smile became a frown.

"Sounds like a wonderful recipe to me," I said.

Ally's face crumbled like a sugar cookie and her shoulders began to shake. "Someone died," she cried.

"At the party? Someone died?"

She wrapped her arms around herself and nodded.

"An allergy to peanuts?"

She nodded again.

I put my hands on her shoulders. "But Ally, you didn't know these people. You had no idea someone was allergic to peanuts."

"Yes, I did know. Zach had told me not to use peanuts. Everyone in his dorm knew that this sophomore Emily was allergic. She carried around one of those EpiPens, just in case."

"But Emily had her EpiPen with her, didn't she? That would have saved her, right?"

"Yes, she had it with her. But it didn't work. She couldn't breathe, and the paramedics took too long. She died on the way to the hospital."

"So then what happened?"

"The police investigated. When they checked the food, there they were—tons of peanuts in our cookie bars. We were all standing around, and Zach was stunned. I was stunned. He kept insisting that we had used absolutely no peanuts. But there they were in the bars. There was no denying it."

Ally was visibly shivering now, and I took off my jacket and put it around her shoulders. "I'll never forget the disappointment in his eyes, believing that I put peanuts in those bars."

"Well, did you?" I asked. "Put peanuts in the bars?"

Ally flinched as if I had slapped her across the face. "No. Of course not. My father is deathly allergic to peanuts. I know what happens to a person with anaphylactic shock. I would never do that.

"When the police said that they would have to arrest us, Zach was the one who took the entire rap for it. He told them that I didn't know anything about it. So they handcuffed him, took him down to the station and booked him."

"You just stood there and let them arrest Zach?"

Ally's head was down and her shoulders were shaking. "That's what hurt the most. He really thought I defied him and put peanuts into those bars. Every time I tried to tell him I hadn't done it, Zach would cut me off and shake his head. He couldn't even face me." She lifted her head, her eyes now red and streaming. "Trudie, please believe me. I didn't do it, but Zach was so sure that I had that he turned himself in. He thought he was protecting me."

"Well, if he didn't do it and you didn't do it, then who put the peanuts in the dessert bars?"

She shook her head. "I don't know."

"After Zach was arrested, did you go to the police then to tell them that he didn't do it?"

"I—I was afraid. I didn't want either of us to go to jail. I didn't think they'd believe me. So I called Daddy, told him that Zach had been arrested for something he didn't do and asked him to help."

"How could your father help Zach?"

"He called his lawyer who was able to get Zach off on a technicality. But that arrest will be on his record forever."

The revelation dawned on me as if I'd opened the refrigerator and the light had come on. "Zach has a record! So that's why they took him in for questioning. Detective Goldman suspects him of doing the exact same thing to your father. Now it all makes sense. I have to call him so they'll take the suspicion off of Zach."

"No, Trudie. You can't do that." Ally's tears had dried a little too quickly. "Then I'll be arrested for Emily's murder. They'll think I did it."

"Ally, don't you want to help Zach? After all he's done for you. Every time you need his help, he comes running." I glared at her, hoping she would realize I knew about the abortion.

She slid back from me on the vinyl bench seat. "What did he tell you?"

"Enough to know that Zach was not the father of your baby, even though you convinced him he was."

The waiter approached our table. "Anything else, ladies?"

"No, not another thing." I grabbed my jacket from Allison's shoulders and stalked out of the bar.


THE STEAK TASTED wonderful, but after meeting with Ally, I couldn't enjoy it. I was furious with her for the way she had treated Zach. But I was angry with him as well for allowing her to knead him like bread dough, let him rise and then punch him down again and roll him flat. Not just once, but over and over again.

What should I do? What could I do? I didn't want to get Ally in trouble with the law, but I would not stay silent and let Zach go to jail. For now, there were no decisions to make. The autopsy results had not come back yet, and until then, no one would know the cause of death. I would take it one step at a time.

In the past few days, my life had turned upside down. I needed to feel grounded, to get a dose of normal everyday reality. I picked up the phone and punched in my mother's number. The voice mail recording answered instead. I'd forgotten my parents were still on their cruise, somewhere in Alaska. I wanted to scream.

The phone rang. What now? I wondered. After a day of confrontations with Zach, with Barbara Lewis, with Detective Goldman and Ally, who else wanted a piece of me? I took a deep breath and pushed the talk button.

"Hi, Trudie." I heard the smile in Bradley's voice. "I just wanted to see how you were doing? Saturday night was pretty traumatic for you. Have you had a chance to blow off some steam?"

"Bradley. So nice to hear a friendly voice. It's sweet of you to call." Phone to my ear, I sank back against the sofa pillows and put my feet up.

"So have you?"

"Have I what?" I asked.

"Blown off some steam?"

"I was just trying to find a way to do that, but there was no one left to call."

"Well, here I am," he said. "Go right ahead. Blow."

I giggled. "What are you doing right now?"

"I'm talking to you," he said, chuckling.

"No, I mean are you standing in your kitchen or walking from room to room, or watching TV? What?"

"I'm lying in bed watching the classic movie station. Cary Grant and Doris Day."

I could picture debonair Cary Grant and Bradley, both so at ease in their tuxedos.

"What are you doing?" he asked me.

"I'm talking to you." I giggled again.

"You know what I mean."

"I'm on my sofa watching some CSI episodes I missed."

"And what are you wearing? I'm picturing a slinky black cat suit. Right?"

"Close," I said, thoroughly enjoying this easy, playful banter. "How about pink leopard PJ's?"

"Mmmm." His voice was soothing. "Let me savor that vision for a moment."

"How about you—what are you wearing?" I held my breath, not believing this whole conversation.

"Boxers."

"And?" I'd never had a phone call like this before, verging a little on the naughty side. But it was fun and liberating. After a day like today, why not?

"Just…boxers."

"Ooooh, nice." I bit my lower lip, picturing his bare chest, his muscular arms—around me. The tenseness in my neck and shoulders eased, and I stretched luxuriously. I began to laugh, and so did he. "Thank you," I said.

"For what?"

"For saving the day. For chasing away the bad vibes. For just being there for me. I needed that. I think I'll be able to sleep now."

"It was good for me, too. Good night, Trudie."

"Good night, Bradley."

I got into bed and nestled into my pillow and comforter as if he'd just tucked me in and bent down to kiss my forehead. His call had given me the comfort and peace I'd needed. I fell right to sleep.

# Chapter Ten

My two-inch heels poked through the soggy ground with each step as I made my way across the grass at the King David Cemetery. I could have chosen flats to attend Mr. Schwartz's funeral, but with my charcoal gray A-line dress, they just made me look short and dumpy. The black strappy pumps I wore showed off my calves, which weren't half bad. My left heel sunk into the sodden earth, and I grabbed Zach's arm to catch my balance.

"Whoa, Nellie," he said, holding me upright so I could pull my foot out of the mud. "Am I going to have to carry you?"

"I wish you could, but I guess it wouldn't be appropriate." And he'd probably fall over from the sheer weight, I thought. "I'll just hang onto you the rest of the way."

The morning rain had stopped, and the sun was beginning to emerge from behind a cloud. A tented shelter had been erected alongside the gravesite with three rows of folding chairs set on top of a sturdy sheet of canvas. A large group of people had already gathered for the service, and unfortunately, all the seats were occupied. I spotted Mrs. Schwartz and Ally seated in the front row, both shrouded in black, both wearing dark sunglasses, the mother clinging to her daughter's arm.

I walked over to them and gave Mrs. Schwartz a hug.

"Trudie, how sweet of you to come." She let go of Ally's hand and leaned forward to whisper in my ear, her breath smelling like she'd had a Jack Daniels omelet for breakfast. "The autopsy results are finally in. They think someone m-m-murdered my Melvin."

"Oh," I gasped. Thoughts swirled through my head as if it were a food processor. Mr. Schwartz had in fact been murdered, just as everyone had suspected. I wanted to ask how he'd died, but this was not the time or place. "I'm so sorry," I said, patting her hand. Maybe later I'd call Goldman to see what I could find out.

I turned to Ally, but she tossed her hair off her shoulder and turned to speak to the woman seated beside her. Obviously, she wasn't ready to forgive me for the way I'd spoken to her the other day. I was the one who should have been holding a grudge after what she'd admitted to me, the way she'd made Zach the fall guy back in college. Because of her, Zach had a criminal record that he didn't deserve. Honestly, I wouldn't care if she never spoke to me again.


I NOTICED BARBARA Lewis sitting beside Mrs. Schwartz and wearing a black wide-brimmed hat with a veil that covered her eyes. We nodded to each other, and then I joined Zach where he stood to the side of the shelter. I leaned against him for support. He wrapped his arm around my waist, his long, thin fingers spread wide on the front of my torso, almost touching my breasts. What the Hellman's was he thinking? I grabbed his hand and pushed it away, worried that any of my current or future clients might be watching. I certainly didn't want anyone to think he was more than just my business partner, but the service was about to begin, and it was too late to move.

I shifted from one leg to the other. My feet, moist from the walk through the grass, were now sliding down in my shoes and squeezing my toes against the straps. There would surely be blisters tomorrow.

The rabbi spoke about Mr. Schwartz, who had been a generous donor to the synagogue. He'd also been a hands-on volunteer, serving meals at a D.C. soup kitchen and delivering toys and books to a women's shelter.

Who would want to murder such a wonderful man? I pulled a wad of tissues out of my purse and dabbed at my eyes, trying to keep my mascara from running.

As the rabbi began to chant prayers in Hebrew, I scanned the crowd, recognizing some of the Schwartzes' friends from the party. There must have been close to a hundred fifty people who'd come to say farewell to Mr. Schwartz. Turning to get a better look, I was surprised to see Bradley. What was he doing here? He had no connection with Mr. Schwartz except that he might have been one of the last people to speak to the man. Bradley grinned at me, his teeth sparkling white against his tanned skin. Always the fashion model, he wore a black blazer, gray trousers and a black and gray striped tie. His broad shoulders filled out the jacket, and I flushed at the thought of our provocative phone call the other night. I turned away and fanned myself with the program.

Looking in another direction, I spotted Detective Goldman standing in a military style at-ease position. I wondered for a moment if he had indeed been in the service or if this was part of his police academy training. He nodded my way, the expression on his face all business. He still wore the same disheveled navy blazer and khakis. Did he have a closet full of them? The man needed someone to take him shopping, I decided, assigning myself to the task.

The rabbi asked if anyone wanted to speak about Mr. Schwartz. After an awkward moment in which everyone glanced around to see who would be the first to speak, a well-dressed man with a charcoal gray pin-striped suit and neatly-coiffed dark hair that was silvered at the temples, stood and walked to the front, facing the guests.

"I'm Bob Lewis," he said in a confident tone.

So that was Mr. Lewis. Now I recognized him from the party, arguing with Mr. Schwartz until his wife settled them down.

"Mel and I did quite a bit of business together over the years," he continued. "I remember him as a young buck right out of college. I took him under my wing and taught him everything I knew about commercial real estate. We bought office buildings together, strip shopping centers. Each time Mel insisted the tenants get their first month's rent free. Always a bone of contention between the two of us." Mr. Lewis chuckled and shook his head. "He was a good man, fair in his dealings, a man of great integrity—almost to a fault." He put a curled fist to his mouth and cleared his throat. "I, for one, will miss him."

Barbara Lewis nodded and smiled at her husband as he resumed his seat behind her.

*Almost to a fault.* I wondered what that meant. How could someone have too much integrity? Had Mr. Schwartz been too honest to go along with some deal? Was there something he'd wanted to expose? Or was I letting my imagination run wild listening to Mr. Lewis' innocent words? This whole situation was making me paranoid. Even so, I would keep my eyes and ears open at the Lewis dinner.

Mr. Schwartz's brother, followed by a friend from their Embassy Row neighborhood, spoke glowing words about him. Then the rabbi asked everyone to stand and recite the Mourner's Kaddish. I opened my program to follow along. *Yit'gadal v'yit kadash sh'mei raba.* "May His great Name grow exalted and sanctified," the English translation explained.

Like most Jewish children, I had gone to Hebrew school for several years until my Bat Mitzvah at age thirteen, where I had recited my Haftorah portion with perfection. Since then, however, my Hebrew had become rusty, and I found it easier to read the transliteration on the left side of the page.

Behind me, I heard Zach chanting the prayer perfectly and knew he had no need to refer to the words in front of him. *Yit'barakh v'yish'tabach v'yit'pa'ar v'yit'romam v'yit'nasei.* Although he and I had been in the same Hebrew school class, there was no question as to who had spent more time on the lessons. *...aleinu v'al kol Yis'ra'eil v'im'ru.* Amen.

When the Kaddish was finished, the mourners filed out. As is tradition, each took a shovelful of dirt and tossed it onto the casket, which now had been lowered a bit into the ground. When the shovel was handed to Ally, she began to cry in high-pitched shrieks, "Daddy! Daddy! No!" Bent with wracking sobs, she jammed the shovel into the mound of dirt and hurled a pile onto the casket, then stood, her shoulders heaving.

Mrs. Schwartz reached out to her daughter yelling, "Ally, baby. Don't do this. Please. Please baby, don't." She stumbled forward, almost plunging onto the casket herself, just as Mr. Schwartz's brother caught her.

Zach rushed to Ally's side, brushed the tear-soaked hair out of her face, and escorted her away.

With everything that woman had done to him, how could Zach be so tender and caring? What was I, chopped liver? Beholding the great expanse I would have to traverse by myself in my heels and wondering if I should walk barefoot, I felt someone take my arm.

Bradley. Be still my heart.

"Keep me company?" he asked, looping his arm through mine. He had the uncanny knack of knowing how to make me feel good. And now he'd done it again by pretending he was the one who needed me.

"Of course," I answered, my smile feeling much too big and toothy. As we walked, I tried to put my weight on my toes so that the heels wouldn't get stuck again. Still, a thought kept gnawing at the back of my mind. What was Bradley doing at Mr. Schwartz's funeral?

"Where are you off to now?" he asked when we arrived at my car.

I noticed Zach was busy helping Ally into a black stretch limo.

"To the Shiva house. I'm catering the reception."

"The what house?"

"Shiva. You know. People come to pay their respects to the family. Kind of like a Wake. Except quieter, and there's no body."

"Oh. Need any help?" Bradley's eyebrows knitted together in concern.

He leaned in closer, and I got a whiff of his cologne, the same one he wore last Saturday night at the Schwartz house. It smelled citrusy, but earthy too, and made me tingle in places I shouldn't, standing there in the middle of the cemetery.

"Well, Zach will be there, mainly to keep the food replenished and to clear away dirty plates," I said. "We could use help serving the beverages, but I couldn't pay you anything. I've offered my services for free."

"Of course I'll help. No charge. I'll feel as if I'm finishing the job I never got to do at the Schwartz party last Saturday night." He opened my car door, and I slid in behind the wheel just as Zach was getting into my passenger seat. "Hey Zach," Bradley said, bending lower to peer into the car.

"Hey," Zach answered in an unenthusiastic tone.

"See you there," Bradley said, closing my door.

I pulled out of my space, anxious to get a head start on all of the guests who would be descending on the Schwartz house.

"See you where?" Zach had a scowl on his face.

"Bradley's going to help us at the Shiva house. Judging by the huge crowd here at the cemetery, we're going to need every hand we can get."

"Trudie, we can handle it ourselves. It's not a sit-down dinner. Just some finger foods and pastries. We don't need Bradley."

At a red light, I jammed on the brakes, and we both jerked forward. I turned to Zach. "With all these people, we do need him. He can help serve drinks. What is your problem with him?"

"I don't have a problem with him. I have a problem with you and the way you act around him, getting all smiley and flirty," Zach said, his face a watermelon red.

The light changed to green, I pushed down hard on the accelerator, and the car lurched forward. "The way I act? What about the way you act around Ally? You always have to come to the rescue for poor, poor Ally. When will you learn that she's just using you?"

"Using me? This was her father's funeral. She was upset. Should I ignore that?"

Only a mile from the entrance onto the Capital Beltway, I sped past the slowpokes in the right lane. "There were plenty of people who could have helped her. You didn't have to be the one. As it was, you left me high and dry to walk through the wet grass by myself. Until Bradley came to my rescue." I accelerated some more. "And you know what, Zach? I'm going to let him help whenever he asks."

The shrillness of a siren caught my attention, and I checked the rear view mirror. Lights flashed atop an unmarked car on my tail.

"Shrimp," I said. "Shrimp, shrimp, shrimp. Now we'll never get there in time." I didn't know what I wanted to do more, scream or cry. I composed myself, pulled onto the shoulder and rolled down my window. "Zach, the registration is in the glove compartment. Would you get it?"

"Lady, do you know how fast you were going?" a familiar voice inquired.

I turned to the window. Detective Goldman. "What are you doing, pulling me over? You know I have to get to the Schwartz house before the crowd arrives."

He nodded at me, "Miss Fine," and then to Zach, "Mr. Cohen. Just doing my job. Again, do you know how fast you were going?"

"I don't know, thirty-five maybe, forty."

"How about fifty in a thirty-five mile zone. I'm going to have to give you a ticket." Between Zach and Goldman, my head felt as if it was sitting in a pressure cooker, the lid about to burst.

"A ticket? You're going to give me a ticket? One day you take me to lunch and the next, you give me a ticket? And since when does a homicide detective give out traffic tickets?" I turned to Zach for confirmation, but he was staring straight ahead, acting invisible.

"Makes no difference when you're breaking the law," Goldman continued, drawing my attention back to him. "I've been following you all the way from the cemetery and could barely keep up. We don't need two funerals today." He pulled out his pad, the same one he'd been using during his investigation.

"You were following me all the way from the cemetery? Isn't that considered stalking? Maybe I should be reporting you to the police." Hah, I thought. I've got him there. "Listen, Detective Goldman, I have to get to the Shiva house, for God's sake. They're waiting for me. Why don't we call it a wash—I won't report you if you don't report me."

"First of all, I was not stalking you. I'm headed to the same place you are. Second, that's bribery, which is an even more serious offense than speeding." He grinned at me and crossed his arms. "But I'll let you go with a warning this time." He gave me a wink. "See you over there."

I watched through my side view mirror as he headed back to his car and pulled out into the traffic. I followed behind.

"He took you to lunch?" Zach asked.

Whoops. I forgot that Zach didn't know about Goldman's visit to the office the other day. "Well, he didn't actually take me to lunch. He wanted to ask a few questions, it was lunch time, and I was hungry. So we went to the Silver Diner. That's all."

"You mean the day I went out to get our salads, came back and you were gone?"

"That would be the day." I kept my eyes forward on the road ahead.

"You didn't say anything about Goldman."

I could feel his eyes boring through me.

"No, I didn't. I don't need to tell you everything that goes on in my life." I thought I sounded pretty convincing.

"But Trudie, we don't keep secrets from each other."

When I stopped at another red light, I turned to him. "If you had said that last week, Zach, I would have agreed with you one hundred percent. Am I supposed to believe that you've never kept anything from me?"

"Okay, except for the stuff about Ally, I've always been truthful with you. Don't you believe that?"

I thought about the peanut incident that had caused a young woman's death, a fact I had just found out from Ally. Something Zach had conveniently never mentioned. Then I glared into his eyes. "No. I. Don't."

ALTHOUGH ANXIOUS TO get to the Schwartz house, I wasn't too worried about being late because May, a former classmate from Johnson and Wales, had agreed to deliver the platters for me. May was short for her given name, Maybelline, her mother's favorite drugstore cosmetic brand when she had given birth to May at age fourteen. May spent most of her childhood and young adulthood overcoming that name. Now, she ran a successful restaurant called, of all things, *Maybelline's*, featuring New Orleans cuisine with an elegant twist. She and I occasionally helped each other out, and I knew she would have everything under control.

I hadn't seen her in a few months, so when I walked into the Schwartz kitchen, I felt the usual awe she inspired. Slim and graceful, May had the complexion of crème caramel. When she glided across a room with a serving tray, her posture erect, her chin held high, all heads turned. Her beautiful and commanding presence could easily have intimidated everyone in that room—wealthy magnates and politicians alike. But May exuded a warmth that immediately put people at ease.

"May, I desperately need your help tomorrow," I had pleaded when I'd spoken to her the day before.

"Shuga," she'd replied in her Louisiana drawl. "Of course I'll help you. It's a weekday, and I am free as a bird."

Seeing her now in the Schwartz kitchen, I gave her a big hug. I could have wrapped my arms twice around her slim frame. "I've missed you. Thanks so much for helping me out. I really wanted to be at the funeral."

"No problem. Listen, it's always good for my business to show off my stuff to potential diners. See," she said, pointing to some platters waiting to go out, "I've added a few of my own specialties."

"May, not your famous Maybelline's Pralines?" I plucked one from the silver tray and popped it into my mouth.

"Stop that, Trudie." She slapped my hand playfully. "These are for the guests. I know they're your favorites, so I've wrapped some up for you over there. Now hands off and let's serve these babies."

In the car, I had changed into my comfortable—and dry—flats, so entering the living room beside May, I must have looked like a duck waddling next to a graceful swan. We circulated among the guests with our trays while Zach kept the tables tidy, removing dirty plates, and Bradley served drinks. We were a good team, like a stew simmering all day on the stove, melding our flavors together.

I noticed Goldman speaking to various people, probably pretending he was a guest making casual conversation. Many, however, most likely recognized him as the detective at last week's crime scene.

"You're not actually conducting interrogations while the family is sitting Shiva, are you?" I asked, pulling him aside.

"No, just playing the field. You know, the killer is right here in this room."

I whipped my head around, jolted out of my comfort zone. "Where? Who?"

"I'm not exactly sure. But the murderer always returns to the scene of the crime. He—or she—is here all right. Isn't that the way it happens on TV?" His wry grin gave him away.

I swatted him on the arm. "You're mocking me again. But seriously, how did Mr. Schwartz die?"

"Anaphylactic shock."

I shouldn't have been surprised. In the back of my mind had been that constant worry that something in our food had caused his death. Or that our guests would forever have that perception of our catering service. Still, remembering what Ally had told me, I began to tremble. "Peanuts?" I asked.

"Yep."

"Then how could you suspect murder? Mr. Schwartz just ate something he shouldn't have." I tried to sound reasonable.

"Did any of your catered food have peanuts in it?" he asked.

"No, of course not." He didn't suspect me, did he? "Mrs. Schwartz gave me strict instructions that no peanuts or peanut oil was to be used. And Zach and I were very careful with all the ingredients and the preparation." I swallowed, thinking back to every dish we'd served. Certainly, Mr. Schwartz had barely touched our food.

Goldman nodded. "And if not you, who?"

Obviously, I thought, someone who knew about Mr. Schwartz's allergy and still gave him peanuts in some form to ingest. The murderer. "But his head was bleeding. Couldn't he have died from the blow to his head? Or maybe he drowned when he fell into the pool."

Goldman shook his head. "Autopsy results don't lie."

Of course, I knew that. In this case, I just didn't want to believe it.

Goldman continued. "Someone wanted him dead, knew he was allergic to peanuts, and assumed that once the food was eaten, there wouldn't be any evidence."

"Assumed there wouldn't be any evidence? You mean there could still be evidence, even after the food has been eaten?"

"Sure. Residue, greasy finger smudges, food samples, any number of things. We gathered it all at the crime scene." Goldman sounded pretty self-assured, but I had my doubts.

I headed toward the kitchen feeling numb. Could Ally have been involved in her own father's death? And could Goldman prove it? If so, would she allow Zach to take the blame for her—again?

I turned my attention back to the detective. Yes, he could be condescending and smug and downright sarcastic, but he was also smart. Surely he wouldn't suspect Zach of murder. Opening the front door, Goldman nodded to me and left. I suppose, even in his line of work, he realized this was not an appropriate time for an official investigation. After the few confrontations I'd had with the detective over the past week, however, I guessed he was making a mental list of people he wanted to question later.

I walked across the room to clear some plates from a sofa table behind Mr. Lewis and another man, who I recognized as a guest at the Schwartz party.

"Bob, listen." His friend spoke quietly. "I hope you've discarded those pants by now. You need to get rid of the—you know."

"You worry too much, Mason. They're good linen pants. I'm having them sent out to the dry cleaners." Mr. Lewis swirled the ice in his glass and then kicked back the rest of his cocktail. He frowned when he noticed me, then handed me his glass.

I froze. He had to know I'd overheard them. "Th-thank you," I stammered. "Would you like another?"

He shook his head, his eyes not leaving mine as he rose from his seat. "I was just leaving."

"Okay. And what about you, sir?" I said to his friend.

"No thanks." His expression was not much friendlier than that of Mr. Lewis.

Once they had gathered their wives, said their goodbyes to Mrs. Schwartz and left the house, I breathed a sigh of relief. Why was it important for Mr. Lewis to get his pants dry cleaned? Was it evidence he needed to get rid of? I wondered if this was something I should report to Detective Goldman. Or was I again letting my imagination get the better of me?

When the guests had gone and May and Bradley were finally convinced to go home, Zach and I stood side by side wiping the last of the serving platters. I gazed at him with a sheepish look, and he grinned. We'd been friends for so long that we hardly needed to speak. We'd made it through another successful catering job. The guests enjoyed the food. The hostess was thankful. What more could we want?

"I'm sorry, Trudie." He peered at me over a clean stack of plates.

"No, I'm sorry. I shouldn't have been upset with you for helping Ally. You did the right thing. It was sweet of you."

"And I shouldn't be jealous of Bradley. You were right; we did need him today. He's just so damned helpful, always smiling like he's posing for a magazine ad. He seems like a nice guy, but I'm not sure yet if I totally trust him."

I walked over to Zach and put my hand on his. "I appreciate your honesty. And I promise that Saturday night at the Lewis dinner, I'll try not to get all 'smiley and flirty' with him. Okay?"

He nodded. "Okay."

"Pssst. Trudie." Mrs. Schwartz stood in the kitchen doorway and crooked her index finger at me.

It reminded me of the story *Hansel and Gretel* when the witch keeps checking the children's fingers to see if she'd fattened them up enough yet. But they tricked her by holding up a bone instead. Mrs. Schwartz's finger looked like that bone.

"Can I speak to you privately?" she asked, slurring her words.

"Sure." I imagined it might have something to do with her whisper to me at the cemetery.

I followed her into the living room. Her feet were bare, and her legs thin as twigs below the black, knee-length dress, as she tottered precariously across the room. She sat down and patted the cushion beside her on the sofa, a gesture for me to join her. Then she leaned toward me. "Tell me, Trudie. You were here last Saturday. Who do you think wanted to kill my dear, dear Melvin?" Every word expelled a puff of bourbon breath.

"I—I don't know. I was in the kitchen most of the time, preparing the food." I had some suspects lined up in my mind, but I wasn't ready to reveal those thoughts to anyone yet. "What do you think?"

"Don't tell anyone, but I think," she started, swaying from side to side. "I think…" and with that, she passed out, falling sideways on the sofa, her head cushioned by a pillow. I stood up, lifted her feet onto the couch, and covered her with a plush throw from the side chair. I checked her pulse and held my hand up in front of her open mouth to make sure she was still breathing. I couldn't afford to lose another client.

What could Mrs. Schwartz have wanted to tell me? Did she have information about something that had happened, something she shouldn't have seen? Or had Mr. Schwartz confided in her about a bad deal that was bothering him? After all, he was a man of great integrity, *almost to a fault*. Whatever it was, I would have to speak to her when she was in a more sober state of mind. How I would accomplish that, I didn't know.

More than that, how was I going to face Mr. Lewis at his dinner party Saturday night?

# Chapter Eleven

Zach and I arrived at work early Saturday morning to take the van to Restaurant Depot in Alexandria. For small restaurants and catering businesses like ours, this was the best place to purchase high-quality meats and produce at good prices. On the way back, we went through D.C. to the Maine Street wharf to pick up the freshest seafood available. Everything was to be low carb as Barbara Lewis had requested for her husband. This would be a no-brainer for me.

By nine-thirty, we were back at the shop beginning our prep work, marinating the flank steaks, steaming carrots and parsnips to puree later, and piping dark chocolate Ls—for Lewis—onto parchment paper to be used as garnish for the brandy-poached pears with cinnamon whipped cream. We'd use the Lewis' linens, china, glassware and silver, which would make our job a lot easier.

In the afternoon, we changed into black shirts and pants, over which I would wear my purple apron with *A Fine Fix* embroidered tastefully in orange italics across one of the pockets, and Zach would wear a purple tie. We had four uniform options that were tailored to various events, some casual and some for dressier occasions. Bradley would be wearing his tuxedo, so I brought along a purple bow tie for him.

Since the dinner party was scheduled for seven o'clock, we arrived at four sharp for our on-site setup. I was pleased to see that the Lewis' housekeeper had already set the table. It would have taken us a good half hour or so to set twenty places with all the china and silverware placed in perfect alignment. Bradley, who arrived soon after us, surprised us by folding the napkins into a fan shape on each dinner plate.

At six, Barbara Lewis swept into the kitchen in a billowing black kimono-style robe. "Trudie, dear," she sang out, surveying our work in the kitchen. "How are things coming?"

"Just fine, Mrs. Lewis. You remember my partner, Zach, and Bradley, our bartender."

"Of course," she said, making her way to Bradley, who was wiping glasses and setting up the bar. "So very nice to see you again, Bradley." She leaned toward him, exposing some cleavage.

Zach glanced at me and shook his head almost imperceptibly, the expression on his face saying, "See? When Bradley's around, I'm invisible."

Bradley gave her his most charming grin. "Mrs. Lewis," he said, taking her hand.

Barbara Lewis giggled, or what might be the sound Queen

Elizabeth would make if she in fact giggled. Then she went into the dining room to set out the place cards.

"What is it about you, man?" Zach asked Bradley after she'd left the room. "You've got every woman wrapped around your finger, ready to do whatever you ask."

I stiffened, afraid Zach was starting a confrontation. He and Bradley were like vinegar and oil in salad dressing, the oil constantly floating to the top, and me always attempting to whisk them together.

Bradley's laugh was edged with bitterness. "For me, it's more a curse than a blessing. Bequeathed to me from my old man."

I remembered my conversation with him at the Schwartz house and Bradley's animosity toward his father, who had wounded his family with his repeated acts of infidelity.

Zach appeared perplexed.

"Sorry, Zach. Believe me, I'm not asking for the attention." He paused, studying Zach for a moment. "Hey, I've been watching the way the two of you handle those knives. I've never been able to get the knack of chopping vegetables like that. Do you think you can show me the technique some time?"

I held my breath, waiting for Zach's answer to Bradley's attempted peace-offering.

Zach frowned then nodded. "Sure. I'll be glad to. Drop by the warehouse whenever you want."

When they fist-bumped, I relaxed and turned back to preparing the shrimp cocktail sauce. I smiled to myself. Maybe the two of them could learn to get along after all. It sure would make my life easier.

"Hello." The deep booming voice made me jump.

Mr. Lewis stood at the kitchen doorway, dressed for the evening in a pale blue shirt and navy blazer with brass buttons. His eyes widened when he saw me. I guess his wife hadn't enlightened him about the catering crew tonight. He recovered quickly from his shock, but frowned as he headed to the bar. "Just want to go over the liquor for tonight with the bartender."

Zach and I continued preparing the hors d'oeuvres. I hadn't told him or anyone else about the conversation I'd overheard during Shiva. As Mr. Lewis spoke with Bradley about the cocktails his guests preferred, my hands shook trying to thread the chicken satay onto wooden skewers.

While preparing the peanut sauce, I stopped stirring.

Peanuts. That was the cause of everything. The death of a college student leading to Zach's arrest. The death of Mr. Schwartz. But it wasn't just the peanuts, was it? The real culprits were the people who had served them up, whether inadvertently or maliciously. Someone, possibly Ally, had put peanuts into those bars the college girl ate. And someone had intentionally given peanuts to Mr. Schwartz.

The question was who? I had been careful not to use anything at the Schwartz party that had peanuts, peanut oil or that was packaged in the same warehouse as a peanut. So who gave Mr. Schwartz peanuts? Was it Ally, his own daughter? Was it Mr. Lewis or one of his business associate? And why was Mr. Lewis concerned about getting his pants dry-cleaned?

The smell of the peanut sauce was beginning to nauseate me. If I never saw another peanut, that would be fine with me.

A little before seven, Barbara Lewis entered the kitchen for a final check. She wore a green and gold silk kaftan and gold chandelier earrings. Her blond hair was swept up with a few loose tendrils dangling on her neck.

"You look lovely, Mrs. Lewis," Bradley said, smiling. "What can I get for you?"

He had it, I thought, and he definitely knew how to use it. I glanced at Zach as he arranged the endive canapés stuffed with herbed cheese, smoked salmon and caviar on a tray. There was no trace of jealousy or resentment and, in fact, he was grinning.

"How sweet," Barbara Lewis cooed to Bradley, touching his cheek. "A chardonnay for me and Scotch on the rocks for Bob, please." She headed toward the foyer when the doorbell announced the arrival of the first guests.

"Okay. Game on. Let's go," I said, beaming at my team. We were ready.

The cocktail hour and dinner were flawless. Elsa, the Lewises' housekeeper, helped to serve and clear dishes, which was a big help with a table of twenty diners. I recognized some of the guests, notably the head of the D.C. City Council, a local TV news anchor, and a bestselling author who lived in Georgetown.

During the meal, Barbara Lewis whispered how pleased she was with my low-carb menu and said she couldn't wait to inform her guests about it at the end of the meal. Everyone raved about our creamy wild mushroom soup and murmured with appreciation at the plating of our entrée, the twin carrot and parsnip purees in the center forming a yin and yang design, surrounded by slices of the grilled flank steak and Brussels sprouts that had been halved and then sautéed with bacon, shallots and garlic. The dark chocolate Ls that stood at attention on each dessert were the biggest hit of all, surprising and delighting Mrs. Lewis.

Although I'd helped with the serving, most of my time was spent in the kitchen, preparing and plating the meals. The first time I entered the dining room, I noticed Mason, the man who'd been sitting with Mr. Lewis at the Shiva house who had asked him whether he'd gotten rid of his pants. He didn't seem surprised to see me. Mr. Lewis must have warned him that I was there, and every time I entered the room, Mason glared at me.

During the evening, several guests asked for my card, including the news anchor. Hallelujah, I thought. We needed the business. Especially wealthy, prominent customers like these. It was a dream come true, and I wanted to kiss Barbara Lewis for giving me this chance, not that boosting my business was ever her motive for hiring me. I still wasn't exactly sure why she'd chosen me. Maybe she had been impressed by the food. Or, more likely, her previous caterer had backed out at the last minute.

Now, as I served dessert to Mason, his wife remarked, "We'd love to use your services some time. Do you have a card?"

I froze. Her husband had been glowering at me the entire evening. I was sure he didn't want me in his house.

"I…I don't believe I have any cards left," I stammered. I was always stammering around this man. "I'll have to check in the kitchen." She could always get my number from Barbara Lewis, but I was sure Mason would nix the idea of using my services anyway.

After dessert, the men moved into the study for brandy and cigars, and the wives went into the drawing room for sherry and chocolates. Elsa was helping Zach and Bradley load the dishwasher and clean up the kitchen. So I took the opportunity to excuse myself and went to the powder room located off the kitchen at the base of the back stairs.

When I came out, I contemplated the carpeted steps that led to the second floor. I knew it was against all reason or sense for me to enter my clients' personal living space. I could get into big trouble; maybe lose my business license, not to mention prospective clients. But I couldn't help thinking about those pants that needed dry cleaning. Maybe they would provide an answer to Mr. Schwartz's untimely death. But after an entire week, would they still even be in the house? Everything in my being told me to stay put, but still I headed up, the carpeting silencing my footsteps.

At the top of the stairs, the entrance to the master suite beckoned me forward. I opened the double doors just enough to slink into the spacious suite before closing them behind me. A California king bed occupied the center of the room, a crystal chandelier hanging directly above from a twelve-foot ceiling. To the left was the entrance to a master bath, dressing area and a closet the size of my bedroom. One peek inside indicated that it belonged to Barbara Lewis. I turned around, padded to the other side of the bed and entered another huge bathroom, dressing room, and Mr. Lewis' closet, which was as well-organized as a platter of sushi, all the jackets lined up together, pants, shirts, shoes, everything in its own category.

There must have been thirty pairs of pants hanging, colors ranging from creams to tans, grays, browns, blues, blacks and plaids. Not to mention the jeans. How would I ever find the pair of pants I was searching for, the one that was being sent out to be dry-cleaned?

Wait a minute. A pair of pants waiting to be dry-cleaned wouldn't be hanging up. They would be in a hamper of some sort. I surveyed the closet. On the left side, several dark cherry wood dressers most likely housed his underwear, socks, ties, cufflinks and other accessories. Beyond the last dresser three brown wicker lidded baskets lined the wall. I opened the first to find his white laundry, socks and underwear. The second housed his dark clothing ready for the wash. I removed the lid on the third basket. Bingo. Dry cleaning.

I was skeptical that in this house, with a housekeeper, a whole week's worth of dry cleaning would not yet have been sent out, but it was worth a try.

On the top were business shirts and trousers as well as a couple of neatly folded suit jackets. What I was looking for would most likely be near the bottom of the basket. Sure enough, the final item of clothing was a pair of off-white linen trousers, just the sort of thing he would have worn to the Schwartzes' backyard Mexican fiesta.

As I reached in to remove the pair of pants, I heard the bedroom door open. Oh, God. My heart began to pound in my chest. I pulled the trousers out of the basket and threw the other articles of clothing back in, closing the lid.

I frantically searched for a place to hide, but the closet was so well-organized, there just was no hiding place. I sunk to the floor between the dresser and the first hamper, balling up the pair of pants against the wall behind me, and held my breath.

For a moment, I didn't hear anything. Maybe Mrs. Lewis had come upstairs to powder her nose or freshen her lipstick.

Then I heard that deep resonant voice. "It's me," he said. "How are you holding up?" Pause. "I know. Me too, baby. Soon. As soon as I can manage it. We're halfway there." Pause. "What about tomorrow? Two o'clock. I'll tell Barbara I'm going to the club." Pause. "Yes, our regular place. See you then."

I could almost hear my pulse beating in my temples as I plastered myself harder against the closet wall. Please, I prayed silently. Don't come in here. Don't come in here. I shut my eyes tight and held my breath. When I heard the bedroom door close, I exhaled audibly and swallowed back the nausea that had lumped in my throat.

I scrambled to my feet too fast, and feeling lightheaded, leaned against the wall until my equilibrium stabilized. As I bent over to retrieve the pair of pants and hide them under my apron, a pulverized substance like sand poured out of the pockets to the floor. Kneeling down, I cupped some of it into the palm of my hand and brought it up to my nose. Then I licked my finger, touched it to the gravelly pieces in my hand and, knowing full well what they were, took a taste.

Peanuts.

# Chapter Twelve

At two-thirty in the morning, I couldn't sleep. My adrenaline was pumping faster than my blender turned up to the whip option. The dinner had been a great success, and compliments from the guests still buzzed around in my head. This was the sort of clientele I had always dreamed of. I hoped they would start calling soon.

Beyond that, I couldn't stop trembling. Now I understood why Mr. Lewis needed to have his pants dry-cleaned. Could he and his friend, Mason, have murdered Mr. Schwartz? Was I a threat to them after what I'd overheard? And now I had the evidence in my possession. I didn't think Mr. Lewis would ever notice that his linen trousers were gone. He would expect Elsa to send them out with the other dry cleaning. He certainly would never suspect I had them. But remembering the way Mason had glared at me, I couldn't help but wonder if I was in danger.

My worries intensified when snippets of Mr. Lewis' telephone conversation replayed in my head, along with warning alarms proclaiming that I knew way more than I should about too many things involving Mr. Lewis.

He would be meeting a woman at two o'clock this afternoon. Mr. Lewis was having an affair. But with who? "We're halfway there," he had said on the phone. What did that mean? Did it have something to do with Mr. Schwartz's murder?

I hadn't mentioned any of this to Zach or to anyone else. They'd think I was being foolish or blowing things I'd overheard out of proportion, letting my imagination run away with me. I wondered if I should contact Detective Goldman with this "evidence" but was sure he'd laugh at me and tell me I watched too much TV.

The phone rang, and I jumped. Who would be calling at this time of night?

"Trudie, it's Zach."

In all the years I'd known Zach, there'd been only two times he'd called in the middle of the night. Once when he'd hit a dog that had run out in front of his car. I could barely calm him down enough to find out where to pick him up. He'd been too upset to drive. The other time was after he'd lost his virginity with his high school girlfriend. The experience hadn't been what others had built it up to be. He thought maybe he'd done something wrong, but he couldn't call his guy friends for advice. Instead, he'd called his best friend—me.

So I knew whatever reason he was calling now, it was important.

"What's wrong?" I asked.

"I've been arrested for the murder of Mr. Schwartz. Goldman was waiting for me when I got home. I'm back at the police station."

"Again?" What was wrong with that detective? There were other, more viable suspects, so why did he keep picking on Zach? Of course, I knew why. Zach had been arrested before for the same thing. When he'd taken the rap for Ally. "I'll be right down."

"Thanks. And Trudie? I think I'll need a lawyer this time."

"Maybe not, hon. Maybe not."

Dressing quickly and putting my hair up in a ponytail, I folded Mr. Lewis' pants into a plastic bag and left my apartment. I took the elevator down to the basement parking garage. Although lighted by amber spotlights, it was pretty creepy at three a.m. when no one else was around. Shadows lurked in every corner, and I sensed someone watching me.

I sprinted to my car, jumped in and locked the doors, checking the back seat to make sure no one was hiding on the floor behind me. Of course, I should have checked the back seat before I got into the car. Thankfully, no one was there. I exhaled the breath I'd evidently been holding. Goldman was right. I watch too much TV and too many crime shows.

But as I pulled out of my space, I saw another pair of headlights come on farther down the row. I would have to pass that car as I headed for the exit. The other driver turned on his engine and revved it up. Who else would be out at this time of night? Maybe some guy going home from a one-night stand or teenagers leaving a party.

It was a straight shot to the garage exit, so I pushed down as hard as I could on the accelerator and sped past him, my tires squealing. When I reached the street, I saw him in my rear view mirror exiting his garage space and pulling up behind me. Silhouetted against the amber lighting of the garage, and with its headlights on, the car was unidentifiable. I could just make out the shadow of a figure in the driver's seat, someone wearing a baseball cap. But I didn't want to stick around to determine who it was.

Deciding to give the situation the benefit of the doubt, I proceeded toward the police station. I turned right, and the car behind me turned right. I turned left, and so did he. My skin prickled with apprehension. It wasn't my imagination. This person was following me.

I turned right and raced down the street, turning right again at the corner, then left at the next corner, then right again, hoping to lose him. I heard the car following behind, making the same turns, its tires squealing. With no traffic on the roads so early in the morning, I couldn't imagine how I could lose my pursuer. Who was following me? And why? My heart pounded in my chest as I sped through a red light and was almost broadsided by an SUV, whose driver blared his horn as he veered into another lane to avoid hitting me.

Think. Focus. What would they do on TV to lose someone in a car chase? The answer hit me like an oven timer going off in my head. I made another sudden right turn, pulled into someone's driveway and turned off the headlights and the car engine.

I ducked down so the car would appear empty. A moment later, I heard a car squeal as it turned the corner and sped past. I lifted my head a little to peek out the window. It was a black Town Car sedan, the kind VIPs use to escort them around town. I squinted at the license plate, but it was too dark to read. The driver had stopped at the corner as if deciding which way to turn. Finally, he crossed the intersection and continued down the road.

Hah! Watching TV isn't such a waste after all, is it?

I sat up, my whole body trembling. Was it my imagination that I was being followed? I didn't think so. I started my car, but didn't turn on the headlights, and backed out, turning in the opposite direction of the Town Car. Then I headed to the police station.

THIS TIME ZACH was not in the waiting area.

The same detective sat at the front desk, feet propped on his desk.

"I'm here to see Zachary Cohen," I said, breathless.

"Sorry, ma'am. He's in a holding cell right now. No one's allowed back there."

"But I'm his friend, Trudie Fine. You remember me from the other night. Zach called me to come down here. I need to see him."

He shook his head. "Sorry. No can do."

In an authoritative voice not unlike that of Barbara Lewis, I said, "I want to speak to Detective Goldman."

"He's gone home for the night," he said, shaking his head.

"Well, call him and tell him he needs to get back here now. I have evidence that will release this man." If I couldn't sleep tonight, then I'd be darned if I'd let Goldman sleep.

"Sorry, ma'am," the guard said. "Detective Goldman is off the rest of the weekend. He won't be in until Monday morning."

What the hamburger? Goldman had been hounding me all week, and now when I need him, he was home in bed.

I took a deep breath and forced a smile. Zach's freedom was on the line. I had to stay calm so I wouldn't sound like a total loony or a hysterical female.

I'm no ingénue. I know I'm not sexy. But I've been around Ally long enough to know how she manipulates guys to get her way. What the heck. I'd give it a try. I smiled at the guard and batted my eyelashes, while still exhibiting my vulnerable side.

"Please, sir. I have some important information that I'm sure Detective Goldman would want to know. He's been working on this case all week. Will you just call him? Please? I'm sure he'll want to see me." I let my eyes water a bit for effect.

"Oh, all right. But if I get in trouble...."

"I promise, you won't. Detective Goldman will thank you for doing the right thing."

WHEN GOLDMAN ARRIVED forty minutes later, I sat in the waiting area on the same bench where I'd found Zach just a week earlier. On one side of me sat a prostitute waiting for her pimp to pick her up. On the other was a homeless man who reeked of urine and who'd hoped to secure a bed in one of the holding cells. The two of them had become my best friends after telling me their stories of woe.

"Finally," I pronounced, tapping my foot, as the detective

approached me.

Goldman hadn't bothered to comb his hair, and he definitely needed a shave. He wore a Bob Dylan t-shirt, jeans and sneakers. For the first time, he resembled someone in the human species with a life beyond the force. His biceps were impressive, and I could just about make out that six-pack below his fitted shirt. I sucked in my breath remembering that first time we'd met when I put my hand on his rock-hard chest to keep him away from Mrs. Schwartz. What was I doing paying such inappropriate attention to Goldman? Zach was in jail, and I was here to present the evidence that would clear him.

The detective didn't seem too happy to be here. "So what's this important information you have for me?"

"Is there somewhere I can speak to you privately?"

He walked me down the hall to his office, a bleak room with institutional-green concrete walls and a desk covered with papers and folders. His wooden, cushionless chair behind the desk appeared slightly more comfortable than the metal folding chair I was assigned to.

"Okay. I'm listening." His face was serious, not at all the smirking, mocking expression I'd seen before. I realized that as much as I disliked this man, I was beginning to trust him.

I unburdened myself of every bit of information I could muster, from Zach's involvement with Ally, and his accepting the blame for killing the college girl, to all my suspicions about the murder of Mr. Schwartz. I told him what I'd overheard at the Shiva house and showed him what I'd found in Mr. Lewis' closet. I hesitated before telling him about the phone conversation I'd overheard. But as I spoke, Goldman's expression never changed. He was a professional for once, and I appreciated that.

"So," I concluded. "You'll release Zach now, right?"

"It's not that easy," he said, shaking his head.

"Not that easy? I just gave you everything you need to absolve Zach and to solve the case. What about these pants?" I asked, holding the plastic bag and its contents out to him. "These are physical evidence."

"They're inadmissible evidence. Can you prove who these pants belong to? And how do we know that you didn't put crushed peanuts into the pockets yourself? If you had these suspicions, you should have called me. I might have gotten a search warrant and located the pants myself."

His voice grew louder as he spoke. Then he lifted himself out of his chair, yelling directly into my face. "Do you realize you could have gotten yourself into serious trouble if, in fact, Lewis had anything to do with the murder and he discovered you in his closet?"

I cringed under his assault. Heat rushed to my head like mercury in a meat thermometer, and I stood up, furious. "Even if I did call you, by the time you got a search warrant some time on Monday, the pants would have been sent off to the cleaners."

His dark eyes focused on mine. "That may be true, but I don't want you interfering in police business. That's our job, not yours."

We glared at each other a moment.

He sat down and lowered his voice. "And I don't want you to get hurt."

I sat back down, exhausted. I'd been up since six the previous morning and wasn't used to pulling all-nighters. I was running on pure adrenaline and had sprung a slow leak. "What difference does it make to you?" I asked.

He turned away and rubbed his face with both hands, as if wiping away his own frustration, then contemplated me. "I'm interested in you. Okay? Why do you think I stopped your car when you were speeding?"

"Because you like me? Funny way for you to show it."

"I didn't want you to have an accident. So I played traffic cop."

I thought about this a moment. Daniel Goldman was interested in me, wanted to protect me. With all of his mocking and snide remarks, he was acting like a school boy who pulls a girl's pigtails to get her attention. Well now he had mine.

"If you do care about me, help get Zach out of jail. Find the real killer." My voice was almost pleading. "I've known Zachary Cohen most of my life. He's a good person who would never knowingly hurt anyone. The only reason he has a record is because he tried to protect someone he loved."

"Trudie, listen." His tone was low and calm. "You've given me a lot of new information. But no real proof. You don't know that these are the pants Bob Lewis wore to the Schwartz party. You don't know why his friend wanted him to get rid of the pants or why there were peanuts in the pockets. Even if these pants were admissible in court, which they are not, the DA will easily point out all the holes in your testimony."

"But you can still release Zach." I had to make Goldman understand that Zach was innocent; that he had the wrong man. I at least had to get the charges against Zach dropped, even if I didn't have enough proof of Mr. Lewis' guilt. "You brought Zach into the station twice because of something that happened years ago which he wasn't even responsible for."

"You can't prove that either, Trudie."

"But I have a witness. Ally told me…"

"Would Ally tell me the same thing if I questioned her?"

I knew he was trying to be reasonable with me, but why couldn't he understand that Zach was not a murderer and shouldn't even be a suspect? "No. I don't think she would. But don't you see that every minute you have Zach behind bars as the suspected murderer, the real perp is getting away with it?"

"Trudie, I'm glad you came to me with all this information. It will be a great help in my investigation." Goldman covered my hand with his. His touch was warm and comforting. "But the judge on call this weekend is sick, so Zach's bond hearing is scheduled for Monday morning. Nothing and no one is getting him out of jail before then."

"Monday morning?" Zach thought that I would get him out now, this morning. How could I tell him he would be in jail the rest of the weekend?

"Look, he's lucky I was able to pull some strings to keep him here. Otherwise he'd be down at the detention center wearing an orange jumpsuit."

"You pulled strings for him?"

"He's your friend, Trudie. I did it for you."

Unexpected tears sprung to my eyes. He did it for me.

"Now I suggest you go home and get a few hours sleep. Then find a good lawyer. And you're going to have to scrape together some money to post bond."

"How much money?"

Goldman ran his fingers through his hair. "Knowing the judge in session on Monday, I'd say he'll put a fifty-thousand dollar bond on Zach's head.

"Fifty thousand dollars? I don't have that kind of money." I was going to have to call Zach's parents, I realized. They'll be heartbroken about all this.

"It's okay, Trudie. You'll only need to post five thousand, not fifty."

I sighed and then laughed, the kind of laugh that comes from a combination of exhaustion and futility. "I can't believe I'm relieved about having to post five thousand dollars." Five thousand dollars. That was a big chunk of what we made last night. Thank goodness Barbara Lewis had handed me a check at the end of the night for the balance of what she owed us, plus a sizeable tip.

Goldman couldn't allow me back to the holding cell, but he had one of the officers escort Zach to his office for a quick visit. The officer escorted him in, hands cuffed behind his back. His face was paler than usual, his hair more tousled than ever.

I approached him to give him a hug, but Goldman stopped me.

"No contact, Trudie. And you've got five minutes. I'll be watching." He gestured toward the glass window framed into his office wall.

Zach didn't seem surprised to learn he'd have to stay until Monday. I'd forgotten he'd been through this once before. He knew about bond hearings.

"Get in touch with Ally," he told me. "She knows a good lawyer who helped—who can help me."

He'd almost slipped and told me about the last time he'd been in jail. I could have told him that I knew the whole story. But he was miserable enough. That conversation could wait for another time and place. In the meantime, I wasn't anxious to speak with Ally again, but it had to be done.

As Daniel and I headed out to the parking lot, I realized that I still had a problem. Now that I faced the prospect of driving home alone and parking in the basement garage, I was becoming anxious. I turned to Goldman. "Can I ask you a favor?"

He nodded. "Sure."

"Would you follow me home?" Seeing the confusion on his face, I realized he thought I wanted to take him home with me, and not just for brunch. "I think someone tried to follow me when I left my apartment, and I don't feel safe going home alone."

"What? Someone was following you?"

"I think it was a black Town Car. He was parked in my garage, and I had a heck of a time losing him on my way here. It was pretty scary."

"Trudie, why are you just telling me now?" he asked, throwing his hands up in frustration. "Did you get the license plate number? How many people were in the car? You should have reported this as soon as you got to the station. We could have put out an APB for them."

"Sorry. I was worried about Zach, and it took you so long to get here, that I must have put it out of my mind. Anyway, I wouldn't have had to leave my apartment in the wee hours of the morning if you hadn't arrested Zach."

"C'mon," he said, shaking his head. "I'll follow you home."

Goldman stayed on my tail the whole way home and drove into the garage behind me. I was surprised when he parked and got out of his car.

"I'll be fine now," I said. "You can go ahead. Thanks for the private escort."

"Oh no. I'm walking you all the way to your door and checking your apartment for unwanted visitors before I leave." He took my arm and led me to the entrance.

"But it's a secure building. You need a code to get into any of the outside doors." I really would feel safe once I was inside the building.

"Trudie, if someone wants to get to you, they'll find a way to do it. Code or no code."

"Okay. I guess you're right."

We took the elevator up to my floor, and I unlocked the door to my apartment. Even though Goldman motioned for me to wait at the door, I followed him as he checked each room, in the closets, under the bed, behind the shower curtain. It was kind of nice having someone watch out for me like that.

"All clear," he announced.

I walked him to the door and peered up at him, his face unshaven, hair falling in his eyes, those dark bronze eyes that bore into me.

He held my face gently in both hands, leaned down and kissed my forehead. "You're kind of a nut, Trudie Fine."

"And what kind of nut would that be, Detective?"

"One of those uncrackable cases I can't seem to get out of my mind." He lifted my chin and kissed me softly on the lips.

His lips felt good on mine. I reached up and put my arms around his neck, drawing him closer for another, longer kiss, my body charged with a new kind of adrenaline.

"Is this part of the official police escort?"

"Something new I'm trying out," he said, his mouth brushing across mine.

I leaned back against the door with Goldman's body pressing against mine. We couldn't let go, didn't want to let go. I could feel him getting harder as he kissed my mouth, my face, my neck.

Goldman broke away. "No. We can't do this."

I stood there with my mouth open. Huh? Why not? I thought.

He grinned at me, breathing hard. "Don't get me wrong, Trudie. I want you more than anything right now. This is killing me. But if I get involved with a key witness and the best friend of the murder suspect, the judge is going to throw the case right out the window, and I won't be far behind."

"So maybe this isn't such a bad idea." I grinned back, inching toward him. "If it's a good way to get Zach released."

"And me released from my duties as detective," Goldman said, his arm extended to hold me back, then to pull me toward him again. He put his arms around me and planted another kiss. "All the more reason to get this case settled. Something to look forward to."

"Mm," was all I could get out.

As he turned to leave, I touched his arm. "Do you have to go? I'm a little nervous to be here alone." I peered up into those deep golden eyes.

He paused and ran the back of his hand down my jawline, then kissed me again. "No, I don't have to go. I'll stay, but I'm sleeping on your sofa. It's almost morning anyway, and I need to get some sleep. We both do."

I nodded and kissed him back. "Thanks, Goldman."

"Just one more thing," he said.

"What?"

"If I'm going to stay the night, would you please stop calling me Goldman? It's Daniel."

I grinned. "Okay. Daniel."

# Chapter Thirteen

Zach and I stood side by side in the White House kitchen preparing the first course salads for the State Dinner. We frantically drizzled raspberry balsamic dressing over the rows and rows of plated wild field greens as a bell alerted us that the President and his guests were getting impatient.

The bell continued to ring, and I felt a gentle touch to my cheek. I opened my eyes to see Goldman standing over me.

"The phone," he said. "It's ringing."

"Wh—?" Holy smoked salmon! I didn't know if I was more startled to see the detective in my bedroom or relieved that I didn't have to feed all those people at the White House. I pulled my blanket up to my neck and rolled toward the bedside table to answer the phone.

"Trudie, did I wake you, honey?"

"Mom. Are you home?" I sat up. "How was your cruise?"

"Alaska was wonderful. Your dad and I stood on a glacier. Such beautiful scenery you've never seen. We'll tell you all about it and show you pictures when we see you. How are you doing, Trudie? Anything new?"

Anything new? Where should I begin? So much had happened in the past week—the Schwartz party and Mr. Schwartz's murder, the things I'd found out about Ally and Zach, the Lewises' dinner party, Zach's arrest, Bradley, Detective Goldman.

I gazed at Goldman, his hair still damp from his shower and a towel wrapped around his waist. He sat down on the edge of my bed. Seeing him bare-chested and sitting so close to me, I felt my body flush from my head down to my toes. I wondered how long I'd be able to resist him.

"I have so much to tell you, Mom. Why don't I come over to see you and Dad later." Mom knew the Schwartzes, so I'd have to break the news to her gently. Hopefully she wouldn't see last week's newspaper or get the news from her friends before I could tell her. And Zach was like a son to her. She'd freak out about his arrest.

"Great. You'll have dinner with us."

When I hung up the phone, Goldman turned to me. "Are you going to tell her about us?"

"Is there something to tell?" I asked. I'd only been with a few men in my life. None had any interest in continuing the relationship, much less staying the night as Goldman had, even if it hadn't been in my bed.

His intense eyes bore into me. "Do you want there to be something to tell?"

I hesitated, not sure what he meant by that. "Listen, Goldman."

"Daniel."

"Daniel. I'm not sure what I want. Right now, my first priority is to get Zach out of jail and prove his innocence. And you should be out there trying to solve this case. Once my friend is free and clear, then I can think about my own life and what I want."

"Fair enough," he said, with an abrupt nod.

"And I don't want Zach to know anything about what happened between us, at least for now. I mean, I've been fraternizing with the enemy." My voice broke and an unexpected sob escaped my throat. I grabbed for a tissue from the night stand as tears welled precariously. "And he's stuck in a jail cell until Monday."

"Trudie, I'm not the enemy. I want to solve this case, too. But all evidence pointed to Zach, and it was my duty to arrest him."

I shook my head. "That's not true. You could have waited until you had more concrete evidence. It's not like he was a flight risk or anything."

"Ah, but he is a flight risk." Daniel stood up and began to pace. "Listen, I shouldn't talk to you about the case, but I want you to know this." He sat down on my bed again. "Zach and Ally had tickets to fly to Toronto tomorrow."

"What? Zach and Ally? Toronto?" I shook my head again, more slowly, trying to digest this information, my mouth open. "How do you know?"

"Surveillance. Had a warrant and hacked into his computer. Ally purchased the tickets online yesterday morning and emailed a copy of the reservation to him."

For once, I was speechless. How could this be? Zach promised me just two days ago at the funeral that there would be no more secrets between us. He was my best friend in this world. Now I wasn't sure I'd ever be able to trust him again.

Daniel's cell phone rang and he flipped it open. "Goldman here. Yeah...okay...okay. Right." As he spoke, he glanced at me then flipped the phone closed with one hand.

"What? Is it about Zach?"

"Yeah. The judge on call is back at work this morning. He released Zach on bail. You can pick him up any time. And because today is Sunday, you'll have twenty-four hours to pay by certified check. You can do that at his arraignment Monday morning."

"He's free to go? That's wonderful news." I threw my arms around Daniel and kissed him on the lips.

He pushed me down onto the bed, pinning my arms on my pillow, his face hovering directly above mine. A bead of water from his damp hair dropped onto my cheek, and when he chuckled, I got a whiff of his warm, minty breath. "I guess I'm going to have to give you good news a little more often."

Daniel leaned in closer for a long lingering kiss. When he released me, I groaned.

"I guess you will." I grinned up at him, my spirits lifted like muffins rising in the oven.

After Goldman left, I got right down to business and called Ally. For now, I wouldn't mention the plane tickets to Toronto. I needed to get back in her good graces and get the name of the lawyer who'd helped Zach get off once before.

"What do you want?" Those were the first words out of Ally's mouth when she heard my voice.

Okay, this could be a little harder than I thought. I might have to knock some sense into her, kind of like tenderizing a chuck steak.

"I need your help, Ally. Well, Zach needs your help. He's been arrested."

"Arrested? For what?"

I decided that bluntness would be the best way to get through to her. "For the murder of your father. With peanuts."

"What? Where did they get an idea like that? Zach wouldn't hurt Daddy."

"I know that and you know that, but Detective Goldman is convinced that Zach is the murderer. The police keep records. They know about Zach's prior arrest and what happened to that college girl who ate the cookie bars laced with peanuts. Your cookie bars, Ally."

"Trudie, I told you I did not put peanuts in those bars. You're not going to incriminate me, are you? I just can't go to jail. I couldn't stand it. I'd kill myself first."

I wasn't going to let on that I'd already let the cookie bars out of the bag, so to speak. I needed her help and would say anything to get it. "Ally, don't worry about that. Right now you have to get in touch with that lawyer who helped Zach. The bond hearing is tomorrow morning at ten o'clock, and Zach needs him to be there."

"Oh, let me see. His name was Bernstein. That's right. David

Bernstein. He was Daddy's attorney for many years. I'll get his number from my mother."

"Ally, just remember that Zach took a fall for you, a big one. You owe him."

"I know," she said quietly. "I'll see if my mom will help out with the lawyer's fee. Just don't tell the police what you know about me. Okay, Trudie?"

"Agreed." Of course, I wasn't going to tell them something they already knew.

I DRESSED QUICKLY and headed to the police station to pick up Zach, so relieved that he wouldn't have to sit in jail another night. I had to get a few things straight with him. If we were going to remain friends and business partners, he would have to come clean and stop keeping secrets from me. I wanted to know what in the world he was thinking, trying to leave town in the middle of an investigation, and without telling me.

At least it was Goldman's day off and I wouldn't have to face him again at the station. My feelings for him and my loyalty to Zach clashed every time I thought about them. I would have to put my emotions aside for now and take care of business.

I spotted Zach hunched over on the same bench where I'd found him the week before. As long as I'd known him, he'd been hyper about everything, always active, moving from one thing to another, hard to keep still. The boredom of his jail cell must have driven him nuts. Seeing him now, wallowing in defeat, I felt my anger soften like butter set out at room temperature.

"Hey," I said, trying to put a cheerful note in my voice.

He turned toward me and smiled. "What's new, Tru?" This was the way he often greeted me growing up together. As adults, he'd say it whenever things weren't going well to try to cheer me up.

I put on the brightest smile I could. "I spoke to Ally. She'll get the lawyer to your hearing tomorrow."

Zach stood up to give me a hug. "This is going to cost us plenty. I'm sorry, Trudie."

"It's only money. We'll make it up at another gig. By the reception we got last night, some of the Lewises' guests will be calling soon. Besides, Ally's going to ask her mother to pay the attorney fees."

We were both silent for a good part of the drive home. I kept glancing over at him waiting for him to come clean, but he just sat looking blankly out the window.

"What?" he asked. "Something's on your mind, so spit it out."

After all these years, he knew me too well.

"Zach, the only way I'm going to be able to help you is to get everything out in the open. No more secrets." I spoke quietly. "Ally told me about the girl that died from the peanut allergy. She told me everything."

He turned to me, and I knew he understood what I meant. That I knew the entire story and how he had taken the rap for Ally and stood trial for murder.

"You're a good person, Zach. Too good. Ally didn't deserve what you did for her. But that's your nature, and I'll bet if it happened again, you'd do the same thing."

He put his head down and nodded.

"So I'm not going to yell and carry on and scream at you for doing such a stupid thing. But do you know why Detective Goldman arrested you last night?"

Zach looked up at me. "Why?"

"It's not just the fact that you were arrested several years ago for the exact same type of murder. He could have waited to collect more evidence of your guilt. Oh no. You had to go ahead and make plans with Ally not just to leave town, but to leave the country." My voice grew louder as I spoke, and now that I pulled into his parking lot and into a space, I could face him and watch his reaction.

"Leave the country?" The question in his eyes almost convinced me he had no idea what I was talking about. But the proof was in his computer.

"Oh, don't play Mr. Innocent with me, Zachary Cohen. You know exactly what I mean. You were planning to fly off with Ally to Toronto. Tomorrow. When were you going to tell me, your best friend, your business partner? Huh?" I pounded my fist on the dashboard to emphasize each question.

"Toronto? I wasn't planning on going to Toronto—with Ally or with anyone else."

"Don't lie to me, Zach. There have been too many lies between us, and I've had enough. You know that she's already made the flight reservations."

Zach took both my hands in his, and I tried to pull away.

"Trudie, sit still and listen to me."

Reluctantly, I glared into his face.

"Remember the other day at the funeral when I walked Ally to her car to console her?"

"Yes. How could I forget?" It still hurt that he left me standing at the graveside.

"Well, she kept begging me to leave town with her, to get away from everything. She said she would make it all up to me; we'd get married and be so happy together and forget everything that had happened between us."

"Isn't that what you've always wanted?" I asked.

"At one time, when I thought I was in love with Ally, I would have jumped at the chance. But at some point I realized she's not the woman I want to live my life with." Still holding onto my hands, he gently rubbed his thumbs across my knuckles. "You are. You're the one who makes me happy every day as we work side by side."

I stiffened, thinking about Goldman, and hoping that Zach wouldn't find out about our attraction to each other and his spending last night on my couch. "So why did you tell Ally you'd go away with her?"

"I didn't. I just told her things would get better and I'd always be here for her, if she needed me. She must have gone ahead and made the reservations thinking she could persuade me to go. That's the only explanation I can think of."

"And again, Ally Schwartz lands you in jail."

# Chapter Fourteen

After dropping Zach off at home, I headed to Georgetown. It was almost one o'clock, and Mr. Lewis would most likely be leaving soon for his romantic afternoon tryst. The phone conversation I'd overheard while hiding in his closet could only mean one thing. Bob Lewis was having an affair.

I couldn't get his words out of my head. "We're halfway there." What did that mean? Maybe he was in love with Mrs. Schwartz. They'd eliminated her husband, and now they were plotting to kill Barbara Lewis. I had to find out. If my suspicions were correct, this might be the evidence I needed to prove Zach's innocence.

I parked my car down the street from the Lewis house and waited. This could be a total waste of time. Mr. Lewis might have left earlier in the day to go to "the club," as he referred to it. Or he could be at his office or golfing or any number of places.

Still, I waited.

After so little sleep the night before, I was afraid of dozing off. My mind wandered to Goldman. I didn't understand what his motive was in staying the night at my apartment. Was he just being protective or did he really have feelings for me? Guys never treated me the way Goldman had. At twenty-eight, never having had a boyfriend, a girl starts to put up splatter shields so she doesn't get burned by the hot grease.

So what was Goldman's angle? Trying to sort out my feelings for him was like sifting through a bowl of confectioner's sugar. Every time he touched me, I melted right into his arms. I sighed just thinking about his kisses.

The sight of the Lewis' garage door opening jarred me to attention. I checked my watch. One-twenty. A silver Mercedes convertible sports car emerged through the iron gates and headed right past my car. I ducked as he passed but doubted he would notice me, even in my orange Honda. He had no reason to suspect that anyone was watching him and no reason to suspect that I would know anything about his secret meeting, but I wasn't taking any chances.

I pulled onto the street and followed, two cars behind him, not sure exactly which way he was heading. This was my only opportunity to find out the identity of the mystery woman, and I was convinced that her identity played a significant part in the murder of Mr. Schwartz.

Heading north on Wisconsin Avenue, we must have hit every red light. When Mr. Lewis crossed an intersection just as the light turned red, I thought I had lost him. But, a couple of blocks later, I caught up.

We continued through Chevy Chase, into Bethesda, where Mr. Lewis finally pulled into the Hilton Garden Inn parking garage. For some reason, I'd expected the love nest to be at some cheap motel where I could watch their comings and goings from the parking lot. Now I had no choice but to park in the garage and try to make my way through the lobby without being seen. Before leaving my car, I pulled my hair into a ponytail, put on sunglasses and a Food Network baseball cap that I kept on the back seat of my car. Once in the lobby, I sat on a bar stool in the lounge adjacent to the elevators.

At the registration desk, Bob Lewis wore jeans, a white polo shirt, and a red Washington Nationals cap. At least he was a fan of the home team. I guessed this was his idea of going incognito. This was not the wealthy businessman I'd catered to the evening before. He walked across the lobby to the elevators and pressed the up button. Once he'd entered the elevator and the doors closed, I watched the illuminated number change until it stopped at six.

I ordered a Diet Coke and waited. It was just about two o'clock, and I wasn't sure whether the woman he was meeting had already arrived. People came and went, families with cameras heading out for some sightseeing, men holding garment bags with business suits checking in for early Monday morning meetings, and twenty-somethings meeting friends at the bar.

Then I saw her. She also sported a cap, all white, the kind she wore to play tennis. Today, her hair was completely concealed under the cap. Her white tennis outfit had a very short skirt that showed off her long, tanned legs. I would have recognized her anywhere.

Ally.

I turned around and sipped my soda until I heard the ding of the elevator arriving and waited a moment for her to enter and for the doors to close. Then I turned back to watch the numbers ascend...one...two...three...four...five...six...bingo!

There was no point in hanging around the lobby. I had accomplished what I'd set out to do, but my mind was completely muddled. I had been sure the mystery woman was Mrs. Schwartz. But, Ally? Ally was having an affair with Mr. Lewis? Why? He was old enough to be her father. And did that mean they were in cahoots to kill Mr. Schwartz? Again, why?

I HEADED TO the warehouse. Zach had told me the van still needed to be unloaded from the party last night. He'd planned to tackle the task this morning, until Goldman intercepted him with an arrest warrant. I figured I'd give him a break today and do it myself.

The door to the office swung open too easily. I stepped in and stopped short. Files and papers were strewn all over the desk and floor, file drawers pulled out and dumped, tables and chairs in the display area overturned. I rushed to the warehouse door, opened it, and flicked on the light. Most of the heavy metal storage shelves had been thrown to the floor, which was covered with shattered china and glassware. The place had been ransacked. Who could have done this? And what were they looking for? Or was this just a warning for me to back off?

As I descended the four steps down into the warehouse, my legs wobbled like overcooked spaghetti.

In retrospect, I should have called 9-1-1 immediately. Or even Zach. But for my own peace of mind, I needed to see if the walk-in cooler, the pride and joy of our catering business, had also been damaged and if the contents were still intact. Just this past week, we had received a delivery of expensive Russian caviar for a vodka party we'd be catering the following week at a large law firm downtown.

With no sign of movement in the warehouse, I stepped carefully over the minefield of shards toward the walk-in. The aluminum door was dented as if someone had tried to kick it in, but the combination lock sat untouched. My hands shook as I turned the knob on the lock. It took me three attempts to get it open. I flipped on the light switch at the walk-in entrance.

Entering the cooler, I sighed with relief to see the cans of Beluga stacked neatly on the shelf. I opened the freezer door at the rear of the walk-in and that, too, appeared fine.

Then I heard the crunching sound of someone walking across the broken glass, pieces skittering across the floor. The vandal was still here, in the warehouse.

I pulled my cell phone out of my purse to call for help, my hand trembling and wet from perspiration, even in the cold temperatures of the walk-in. The phone slipped to the floor.

The crunching noise sounded closer and louder.

I whirled around just as the cooler door slammed shut.

All went dark.

# Chapter Fifteen

Was I alone? Or had he, or she, followed me in to take care of me once and for all? I held my breath and listened. I could almost hear the pounding in my chest. I waited. Nothing. No one.

I scanned the floor for my cell phone, but the LED had gone black and I couldn't see it. I slid my foot out in front of me, feeling in the dark. Gently, I thought. You don't want to kick it across the floor. Finally, my toe touched something solid. I bent down to retrieve the phone and pressed the menu button. The screen lit up. "Okay, Trudie. You're doing fine," I whispered, trying to calm myself.

I pressed the numbers 9-1-1 and hit the send button. Nothing. I tried again. 9-1-1. Send. No dial tone. No connection. No ringing. No signal in the walk-in. The cell phone went black again.

I needed light. I rummaged in my purse until I found my keychain with the pen light attached, then turned it on and swept it across the room just to confirm that I was, in fact, alone. Alone inside the walk-in, maybe. But who was in the warehouse? I moved to the door and listened. Would I even hear anything out there while stuck in this insulated, aluminum box?

I knew about the safety latch to get out. After all, I'd been in and out of this walk-in cooler for the last year and a half. What I wasn't sure about was what or who I would find once I got out of here. Then I did hear something, a scraping sound of something being dragged across the warehouse floor. Something heavy being moved. The sound became louder and, I realized, closer and stopped at the cooler door. Footsteps, sending fragments of glass and china skittering across the floor, became fainter, moving further from me.

Then silence.

My adrenaline must have been keeping me warm to this point but now, I realized, I was cold. My recollection of when we'd purchased the walk-in was that the refrigerator averages about forty degrees and the freezer a good ten degrees colder than that. Even in my coat, scarf and gloves, it would be pretty chilly. But on a ninety-degree July day like this, I wore only a short-sleeved blouse, cropped pants and sandals. I began to shiver.

I needed help. Zach was at home, probably catching up on his sleep. This was Goldman's day off, and even if he tried to call me, he'd just leave a message. I started to tremble uncontrollably. I was freezing. I had to get out.

I swung the pen light beam back and forth across the door until I located the red plastic knob. Should I open the door or not? I didn't know who'd be waiting for me out in the warehouse.

If I stayed in the cooler, I was doomed to freeze to death. If someone waited in the warehouse to do me harm, I would deal with it then. At least I'd have a chance. I approached the cooler door and located the red knob again with my pen light. Slowly, I put my hand on the knob and pushed it forward. Tears of relief streamed down my face as I tasted my freedom.

The door opened.

It opened barely a half inch, then stopped. It wouldn't budge. Whatever had been dragged across the floor was now blocking the door. Whoever had locked me in wanted to make sure I couldn't get out.

"Oh my God," I said out loud. "This is it for Trudie Fine. I am going to die."

I sat down on the floor and leaned against the cold metal shelves of boxes and jars and cans. I was going to die. I was going to die of hypothermia. I knew from TV shows that I would start to get sleepy, then disoriented. Maybe even begin to feel hot and take my clothes off. And then I would fall asleep—and die. I pulled up my knees and began rubbing my arms briskly to keep the circulation going. It didn't help. I stood up and tried jumping up and down, but I was still freezing. At least the temperature in here would keep my body from decomposing until someone found me.

Poor Mom and Dad would be devastated. I hadn't seen them for two weeks, couldn't hug them or tell them I loved them.

A note, I thought. I had to write them a note. And one to Zach. More than that, I needed to tell Goldman what I'd seen at the hotel. I snatched a pen and scrap of paper from my purse, and using my pen light, my hand trembled as I began to scrawl the things I needed to say. The ink must have been cold because the pen kept skipping. I stopped periodically to scribble on the paper to get the pen working again. Great. They're going to find me dead and wonder why I spent my time doodling when I could have been writing meaningful notes.

Wait a minute, I thought. This is not me. I stood up. Trudie Fine does not just give up. When there's an obstacle she finds her way around it, through it, and out—

—Out.

I pounded on the door with the palms of my hands, yelling, "Help, help! Someone help me." I grabbed a gallon-sized can of Manzanilla olives from the shelf and proceeded to bang it on the aluminum door. I bent over, exhausted, struggling to catch my breath. Who was going to hear me? The warehouse loading dock door was closed. Even so, very few businesses in the industrial park were open on a Sunday.

My body was rigid, my hands white and numb. I rammed my shoulder and hip into the door over and over again, emitting with each thrust a thunderous groan, the same sound I'd used when wielding a cleaver in my butchering class at school.

The sound of footsteps crunched through the shards of glass in the garage. I froze. They wanted to quiet me—for good. I heard them right outside the cooler door, moving the obstacle, scraping it along the floor so that the door would open. I grabbed the heavy olive can and held it above me, ready to knock it over someone's head.

Very slowly, the door opened.

"Trudie?"

"Bradley?"

His eyes were directed up above my head and widened at the sight of the can I was holding. "Whoa. What are you doing with that thing?"

I dropped the can of olives on the floor and threw myself at him. "Oh, Bradley. You saved my life."

He put an arm around me and led me out of the cooler. "What happened? Who did this?"

I leaned against Bradley, panting and basking in the warmth of his body. "I—I don't know. I never saw him." I turned slowly to survey the damage. "It's gone. All gone. We spent three years saving and scrimping and going to closeout sales and surfing the web to build up our inventory. Now look at it." I spread my arms toward the destruction to make my point. "Everything is ruined."

I began to sob, more with the relief of being warm again. Of living to see another day.

Bradley ran his hands up and down my arms, scanning the room to take in the shattered remains of what used to be our entire stock of glassware and dishes. Then he turned to me. "Have you got insurance?"

At first my mind went blank. Zach took care of the administrative end of the business. But then I remembered. "Yes," I said, hope rising in me like bubbles in club soda. "Yes, yes, yes. Zach took out a policy when we opened our doors. He had me cosign the paperwork.

Bradley, you're wonderful." I wrapped my arms around him and gave him an exuberant kiss on the cheek.

"I didn't do anything," he said, laughing. Then he pulled me back to him and kissed me on the lips.

Startled, I took a step back. What was going on today? Did I have some kind of irresistible pheromones? I flushed.

Bradley grinned at me. "Sorry, Trudie. A little impulsive, I guess. C'mon," he said, taking my hand. "I think you have some calls to make." He led me into the office, then picked up my overturned desk chair and helped me into it.

I pulled out my cell phone, but before dialing the police, I peered up at Bradley. "What are you doing here anyway? You've never even been to our office before."

He smiled at me. "Trudie, remember? Zach said to drop in whenever I wanted so he could show me his chopping technique. I wasn't sure he'd be here. Just decided to take a chance." He frowned at me. "And I guess it's a good thing I did."

I studied Bradley's face—his emerald eyes, his chiseled features, dimpled chin, that constant smile. It all seemed too perfect.

A minute later, I reached 9-1-1 and explained my emergency. Then, knowing the Montgomery County police would respond to the call, I also dialed Detective Daniel Goldman, who arrived soon after.

Zach, although distressed about the destruction, was only concerned for me. "We can replace all that stuff," he murmured into my hair. "We can't replace you." He pulled me close and wrapped his long arms around me in a protective hug. I leaned my head against his chest and began to cry softly. It confused me that, of these three men, Zach was the one who gave me the most comfort. After all these years with Zach at my side, he was the cream in my coffee, the syrup on my pancakes, the cheese on my macaroni.

"What are they doing here?" He gestured toward Bradley and Daniel.

I peered up at him through my tears. I could easily explain why Bradley had come and literally saved my life, but there was no way Zach would understand why I'd called Daniel. "It's a long story. Another time."

# Chapter Sixteen

B y this time, the county police had written up their report and were dusting for fingerprints in the office, the warehouse and on the walk-in cooler. Between the investigators, Bradley, Daniel, Zach and me, the office was getting pretty crowded, and Daniel suggested escorting me home safely.

"I'll make sure she gets home," Bradley said, taking my arm. "I'm free all evening."

"If anyone is going to get her home, it's me." Zach took my hand and pulled me from Bradley. "In fact, you'll come to my place, Trudie, where I can keep an eye on you."

"Wait a minute," I said. "What time is it?"

"Five-fifteen," Zach informed me.

"Five-fifteen? My parents are expecting me for dinner." I stood up and began gathering my things to leave.

"Trudie, you are not going out there alone," said Daniel. "Not on my watch."

"Don't worry. I'll follow her," said Bradley, smiling and holding his arm out for me to take it.

"I'll go with her. I know her parents well, and they'll be happy to see me." Zach stood with his hands on his hips, blocking Bradley's way.

Daniel swaggered over and put his hand on my arm. "Trudie needs someone who can protect her, and I can give her a police escort."

I looked from Daniel to Bradley and then to Zach, all three surveying me expectantly.

"Listen," I said. "I can't deal with this right now." I pulled out my cell phone. "Hi, Mom. I'll be there in about twenty minutes. Can I bring a few friends for dinner? Great. See you soon."

"Okay. All of you, follow me. We're all going to my parents' house for dinner."

On a Sunday, my mother always made enough to feed the whole neighborhood, so that didn't worry me. I just hoped she wouldn't faint when she saw who I was bringing for dinner. I could only imagine what the neighbors would think when our caravan of four cars pulled up to my parents' house.

Months seemed to have passed since I'd seen Mom and Dad. It had only been two weeks, but a lifetime of events had taken place while they'd been on their cruise. At the door, I hugged my mother fiercely, so happy to be held by someone I knew loved me for who I was. When we broke our embrace, Zach walked in behind me.

"Zachary, my bubula," she said. He bent down to hug her, and she kissed him on both cheeks. As Bradley entered, Mom stood back. "Oh," she said, her hand over her open mouth, her eyes widening.

Next, Daniel stepped into the foyer.

"Oh my." I heard my mother gasp a little and take another step back. Her face turned as pink as her polyester pants suit.

I couldn't blame her. She'd been trying to marry off her dateless daughter for years. Now I walk into the house with not one, not two, but three attractive men.

"Mom, this is Bradley Miller and Detective Daniel Goldman."

"Nice to meet you, Mrs. Fine." Bradley took her hand and grinned.

She let him hold it a moment and flushed, unable to speak.

"And this is Detective Daniel Goldman," I repeated, to break the spell she'd fallen under.

"Oh my," she repeated, shifting her attention to Daniel. "A detective. Goldman, is it?" She nodded approvingly. "Welcome." She patted her bleached blonde hair as if making sure every lock was in its place.

After making all the introductions again to Dad, my mother escorted us into the living room. "Sid, where's that nice wine we brought back from Alaska?"

In the living room, Mom served us smoked Alaskan salmon with crackers and Dad poured the wine purchased on the cruise ship. He wore navy Bermuda shorts, white deck shoes and a white t-shirt that read, "Size Does Matter" with a map of their Inside Passage route.

With everyone more or less relaxed, I broke the news about Mr.

Schwartz's murder. Bradley and Daniel added their own commentaries to help defuse Mom's distress. Zach sat quietly.

"Poor man," she said. "I remember meeting Melvin at your graduation ceremony. A nicer man you would never meet."

Then I told her about Zach's arrest. "It'll all be fine, Mom, when he's cleared. And tomorrow, at his bond hearing, his lawyer will get everything straightened out."

We all turned our attention to Zach, whose face was now red as cherry Jello.

"But I don't understand why Zachary, such a wonderful boy, would be arrested in the first place," my mother said to Daniel. "We've known Zach since he was six years old. Gentle as a lamb, he is."

A sacrificial lamb, I thought.

"Yes, Daniel. Why would anyone want to arrest Zach?" I asked, enjoying his momentary discomfort as he shifted in his seat.

He cleared his throat. "Well, uh—Mrs. Fine. It seems that the evidence pointed to Mr. Cohen. But just as Trudie says, he is out on bail and of course, he's innocent until proven guilty."

"Detective," Dad said. "What brings you gentlemen here with Trudie tonight?"

"Sid! Goodness. These are Trudie's guests, and of course they are always welcome in our home." Mom gave my father a signal that, after all these years, he knew meant to shut his mouth.

"Just watching out for your daughter," Daniel answered. "As a matter of fact, Trudie, I think you should tell your parents what happened this afternoon." He gave me a smug smile that said, "Let's watch you squirm now."

"Trudie, what happened?" All Mom's attention was on me now.

"Well," I began, searching for the right words. "It seems someone broke into my office and warehouse and did quite a bit of damage."

"Are you all right, baby?" Now my father appeared worried. One priority of mine as a young adult has always been to keep my parents from worrying. Any concern for me on their part meant several phone calls a day and unexpected visits to my apartment. For that reason, I tended to gloss over situations and make light of them.

"Probably some teenagers getting into trouble," I said, shrugging my shoulders. "The police are investigating, and the insurance will pay for the damage." I didn't know exactly what our insurance would cover. Zach and I would have to dig through the overturned files to find our policy and file a claim. Hopefully, we'd get the money soon so we could replenish our lost inventory.

"Well," Mom said, getting up to refill the glasses, "I guess we should be relieved that Trudie has three strong, handsome men to protect her."

"Mrs. Fine." Bradley smiled broadly. "I'm sure we'd all love to hear about your Alaskan cruise. Mr. Fine, did you get to do any salmon fishing?" He leaned forward in his chair as if ready to be riveted by their stories. Leave it to Bradley, the peacemaker, to relieve the tension in the room.

Mom brought me into the kitchen ostensibly to help with the dinner. "Trudie, honey. Where did you meet these delightful men?

How long have you known them?"

"Only a week. Bradley helps us out with bartending, and Daniel is the investigator on the Schwartz murder case."

"Oh, my. Poor Melvin and poor, poor Dana. She must be heart sick. Ally, too." She tsk, tsked and shook her head.

"So much has happened while you and dad were away. I'm just trying to process it all."

Mom glanced toward the living room. "Yes, I can see that. And is there something special going on with any of these men?" She folded her arms, nodded and smiled at me with all the pride of a chef watching his over-achieving protégé.

How could I tell her that there'd been encounters of one type or another with all three of them? And all in one day. I wasn't sure about their feelings or mine, so how could I begin to answer her question? "I-I don't know. Maybe."

She put a gentle hand on my cheek and peered into my eyes as only a mother can. Then she nodded. "Just follow your heart, Trudie, and it will all become clear." She hugged me and kissed my forehead. "Now help me get this food out on the table."

We all sat at the dining room table devouring Mom's delicious brisket with roasted potatoes and carrots. Mom had seated Bradley next to me with Daniel and Zach directly across from us and Mom and Dad at either end. Daniel glared at Bradley with an intensity as sharp as my Santoku. This seemed to have no effect on Bradley, who spent the evening charming my mother with his smile and politeness while listening intently to Dad's musings about the Inuit natives of

Alaska.

"So, Bradley," Mom said, interrupting Dad in the middle of one of his ramblings. "You're single, I gather? What do you think of our Trudie here?"

"Mom!" I couldn't believe she was doing this at the dinner table and right in front of me.

Bradley turned to me and put his arm across the back of my chair. He gazed at me as if I were the cream filling inside a Twinkie. "Trudie is the epitome of womanhood. She is everything a man could ever want. I have nothing but the highest admiration for your daughter, Mrs. Fine."

I glanced at Daniel. If his eyes were lasers, he would have turned Bradley into a pile of ash.

"Oh Bradley," Mom said. "You certainly have a way with words, don't you?"

"And a way with women," Zach added. Up to this point he'd been sitting quietly, brooding, as he often did when things weren't going his way.

Dad turned to Daniel. "And what about you, Detective Goldman? A single man, also?"

Oh my god. Not Dad, too. I wanted to dive under the table.

Daniel was quick to reply, "Yes sir. I am." He gazed across the table at me.

"You're single and Jewish?" My mother's expression turned to ecstasy.

"And looking." He nodded to Bradley. His expression said,

"Touché. Who has the upper hand now?"

"Well I am single and Jewish and I'm outta here." I stood up, plunked my napkin on the table, and stalked out of the dining room, grabbing my bag as I headed for the door. I turned to wave to Mom and Dad and discovered Daniel, Bradley and Zach right on my heels, mumbling their thanks to my parents for a delicious dinner.

# Chapter Seventeen

In my rearview mirror, I saw Goldman, Bradley and Zach playing leap frog with their cars to see who could stay closer to me. I'd had enough of all of them. It had been a long day. My partner was being arraigned for murder tomorrow, my business had been destroyed, Ally was having an affair with Mr. Lewis, and I was being pursued by three single guys, not to mention a murderer. What I needed was someone objective to confide in.

At a red light, I pulled out my cell phone and called May.

"I'm so glad you're home. Can I come over? I really need someone to talk to."

"Of course, shuga. You know I'm here for you any time." Her voice was as smooth and calming as a bowl of Vichyssoise.

I knew my abrupt turn to the right instead of the left had caused some confusion for my three followers when a minute later, Goldman rang my phone. "Trudie, where the hell are you going?"

"I have a stop to make," I said. "Is there some kind of law against that?"

"I'd like to get you home safe and sound," he snapped. "I'm not your personal bodyguard. I can't follow you all over town."

"I don't expect you to follow me around. You're free to go on your merry way whenever you like."

"And let that grinning phony try to protect you? No way."

"That's your decision." I pressed the off button.

MAY STOOD TALL and regal in a silk kaftan of purples, greens and yellows. Her close-cropped hair was dyed burgundy, and gold hoops the size of donuts hung from her ears. When we hugged, she smelled like cinnamon and oranges.

I hadn't been to May's house in quite some time, and as I followed her through the living room, the fabrics in the furniture and draperies, awash in the colors of island spices like paprika and cumin and nutmeg, comforted me.

"What is that wonderful aroma?" I asked, following her into the kitchen.

"Just thought I'd fry up a batch of beignets. Nothin' like sugared dough to lighten your mood."

"May, I didn't want you to go to any trouble for me. I just want to talk." I plopped down at her kitchen table.

"No trouble at all, ma chèrie." She put the puffed and sizzling beignets on a platter and sprinkled them with powdered sugar, then poured us both steaming cups of café au lait.

"You're spoiling me, but I love it." I took a bite, closed my eyes in rapture, and then licked the sugar off my fingers. "No one makes beignets like you."

"Listen, shuga. Did you notice those three cars at the curb with their headlights on?" She nodded toward the window. "One's an unmarked police car, if I'm not mistaken. They might 'a been followin' you."

"They're following me, all right." I laughed, my exhaled breath blowing powdered sugar across the table onto May's kaftan.

"Go on," she said, brushing the sugar off her lap.

"That's one of the things I want to talk to you about. But there's much more to tell." I gave her the whole story, starting from the Schwartz party and the murder up to my business being ransacked with me being locked in the cooler. I left out a few details, including my suspicions of who the murderer might be and Ally's tryst with Mr. Lewis.

"Woo, girl. And I thought I had troubles." She shook her head and patted my arm.

"My biggest problem right now, after I pay Zach's bail and his arraignment tomorrow, is how to keep my business open. How in the world am I going to cater parties without any equipment?"

May stood and refilled our cups. "I think I can help with that one. Listen, remember Johnny Blue, you know, from Blue Fin Caterin'? Last year his place burned down to the ground. Lost everything."

I had read about it in the newspaper, but I thought he was back on his feet now. I'd assumed his insurance took care of it.

"Johnny was in bad shape. Coulda' lost his business, his clients, everythin'. Well, some of us from the U Street corridor—we banded together somethin' fierce. Until Johnny got his insurance money and his place rebuilt, we each loaned him kitchen space to work in, dishes, glasses, linens, whatever he needed."

"Didn't that drain resources from your restaurant, though?" I asked.

May cupped both her hands over mine. "Not at all. Each one gave him a little help or space or equipment to use. No big sacrifice for any of us. And let me tell you, Johnny's business boomed last year, even better than the year before. When he got back on his feet, he was so grateful that he makes it a point to help out strugglin' caterers, the ones that are newly opened but can't afford their own place yet."

"I had no idea."

"So don't you fret about your business, shuga. I have plenty of equipment for you to borrow when you need it. Just concentrate on Zach, gettin' the insurance papers filed and the place cleaned up. If I don't have what you need, I'll find others who can help. We'll all pitch in until you're back on your feet. I've got you taken care of."

Tears welled up and slid down my cheeks. I dabbed at my face with a napkin and smiled at May. "I just wanted someone to talk to, but you've solved half my problems. How can I ever thank you?"

May waved off my appreciation. "Ma chèrie, it wasn't long ago you saved me when I lost my home and my business to those floods in N'awlins. You took me in and helped me get started in D.C. Not somethin' easy to forget."

We clasped hands across the table.

May nodded toward the window. "Seems like some of your problems are still sittin' out there."

"Oh, yeah." I'd almost forgotten about Daniel, Bradley, and Zach. "Between the three of them, I'm so confused. It's all happening too fast, and I have no experience with this kind of attention from men."

"Let's think about this together," said May. "Pretend that all four of you are stuck out on some desert island in the Caribbean..."

"Wait. Could you choose another location? I'd rather not be seen in a bathing suit."

"Okay. Let's see." May tapped her fingernails on the white Formica top. "You've just returned from a long journey."

I leaned forward and rested my elbows on the table. "How long?"

"Six weeks." Her eyes widened. "You emerge from the train, and there they all stand: Zach, Bradley and Daniel. All smilin' and happy to see you. Which one you gonna throw ya' arms around?"

"They're all happy to see me? I'm not sure."

"Shuga, think about them one at a time. Take it slow."

I pictured the scene in my mind. "When I think about Zach, I'm happy to see him."

"Why?"

"Well, Zach's always been there, like a best friend. When I'm with him, I'm usually happy because we're working together, cooking, planning menus, shopping, that kind of thing. But I don't want to run into his arms and kiss him."

"And Bradley?"

I smiled. "When I first met Bradley, I couldn't stop staring at him.

He's gorgeous. He's perfect. When he held me, I tingled. His touch, his scent mesmerized me. But I don't know. There's something too perfect about him, plastic almost. He's like artificially enriched white bread, while I'm pumpernickel."

"Girl, if anyone's pumpernickel around here, it's me, or my name isn't Maybelline Dubois. Shuga, you are whole grain bread through and through. You're organic. You're the real thing. Natural. No artificial ingredients. That's why these men all like you. What's on the label is what they get. In a world like this, there's something very desirable about that."

May wasn't much older than me, but she was wise beyond her years. I knew she was right. Any man who wanted me would have to accept me, and love me, just the way I am.

"Now tell me about Daniel."

I grinned and lowered my head. Heat rose to my face.

May put her hand out and lifted my chin, her feline-green eyes penetrating mine. She nodded. "I think you got your answer. Laissez les bon temps roulez."

"Huh?"

"Ma chèrie, let the good times roll."

A horn honked outside, and we both turned to the window. Daniel was flashing his headlights. I checked my watch. Nine-thirty. I'd been at May's almost an hour.

"Gotta go." I stood up and hugged May. "How can I ever thank you? You've lightened my load, puffed me up like those beignets. Of course, my hips are going to puff up after the three I just ate."

When May opened the front door, there was Daniel getting ready to knock. "It's about time. Are we heading home now?"

I put my hands on my hips. "I'm heading home. Nobody asked you to follow me here or anywhere else."

Bradley approached the door and held out his arm to me, that big Cheshire cat grin on his face. "I'd be happy to escort you to your car, Miss."

Zach stood behind them on the walkway. I sidestepped Daniel and Bradley and took Zach's arm. Then I led my entourage all the way home and into my parking garage.

When they emerged from their cars, Daniel held up his hand to the others. "I've got it covered from here. You can go on home now and brush those pearly white teeth of yours, buddy," he said to Bradley.

The only time I'd ever seen so much as a frown cross Bradley's face was when he spoke about his father. But now his eyes narrowed at Daniel, and I could tell by the movement of his jaw that he was angry.

Daniel must have noticed it, too. "Maybe I was out of line. No harm intended. And thanks, Bradley. You saved our girl's life today." He extended his hand, and Bradley reciprocated. I knew from some of the reality cop shows that Daniel was trying to neutralize the situation before it got out of control. "I'll walk Trudie to the door and make sure she gets in safely. Truthfully, I think she's had enough of all of us for one day. Okay with you, Zach?"

Zach regarded me. "If it's okay with Trudie."

I smiled. "Of course, it's fine. Thanks for your help today. All of you. I'm lucky to have such good friends who care about me."

Bradley and Zach turned and got back into their cars.

Daniel escorted me upstairs, and as before, checked each room for unwanted visitors. Standing at the door, Daniel wove his fingers through my hair and brushed his lips across mine. Then he wrapped a hunk of my hair around his hand, gently tilted my head back, and planted an insistent kiss.

"I've been wanting to do that all day," he mumbled into my mouth.

I clung to him, limp and helpless, unwilling to let go. "Can't you stay for a little while?"

"Better not," he moaned, breaking away. "There's no such thing as a little while if I stay a moment more. Tomorrow. I'll meet you at the courthouse for the hearing."

"Tomorrow," I said.

I closed the door behind him, threw the deadlock and latched the chain. Then I headed for bed after the longest day of my life.

# Chapter Eighteen

I groped for the ringing phone in the pitch dark. The clock read three-fifteen. Who would be calling me at this hour unless it was an emergency?

I finally found the receiver. "Hello?" No response. "Hello?"

"Warmed up yet, Trudie?" a voice rasped.

"What?" I propped myself up on one elbow and scanned the darkened shadows of my bedroom.

"Watch out. Don't get too close." With the voice masked, I couldn't tell if it was male or female. "Next time you won't escape."

"Who is this?" I flicked on the bedside lamp and sat up, listening for more.

The phone went dead.

My heart thumped as if someone was pounding veal inside my chest. I picked up the receiver again to dial Daniel. No, I wasn't going to wake him. He needed the sleep as much as I did. This could wait until tomorrow.

I turned the light off and lay down. Shivering, as if I were back in the walk-in cooler, I pulled the blanket up to my neck. I'd heard of post-traumatic stress and wondered, after my brush with death yesterday afternoon and this early morning phone call, if that was what I had. I wished Daniel had stayed over. What I wanted was to curl up into the warmth of his body and feel the comfort of his arms around me.

THE ALARM WOKE me at seven-thirty. After a quick cheese omelet to fortify myself, I dressed in my power color: a royal purple suit. Having made it through the previous day's events and the threatening phone call during the night, I drove out into the sunlight with a renewed confidence. All I needed was a red cape flowing behind me. I was going to court to rescue Zach—pay his bail and do battle at his hearing.

I stopped at the bank and, based on Daniel's guess, had a five thousand dollar certified check drawn up for bail money. Five thousand dollars would go a long way toward the purchase of the red Viking stove I'd been fondling on a regular basis at the appliance store. Then I remembered all of our damaged equipment we would have to replace even before we saw a cent of the insurance money. Oh, well. As they say, "Easy come, easy go." There would be more gigs, but there was only one Zachary Cohen.

Daniel was waiting outside the courtroom when I arrived. "The hearing is about to start, a little early. I'm glad you're here. Let's go in."

"But I have something important to tell you."

"No time now. You can tell me later." He put his hand on the small of my back and urged me through the carved mahogany double doors into the courtroom.

True to her word, Ally had procured the services of David Bernstein, attorney to the rich and powerful. Facing the judge's bench with Zach beside him, Mr. Bernstein, in his starched white shirt, silk tie and Italian leather shoes, took charge of the bond hearing with finesse.

Zach stood erect and silent and was dressed in a suit he'd apparently pulled from the back of his closet, out-of-date and a little baggy. I wondered whether he'd been eating lately and was glad he'd had dinner at my mother's house last night. Still, he appeared thinner, and his complexion was as gray as overcooked green beans.

The judge read the charges, formally accusing Zach of the murder of Melvin Schwartz. Knowing full well why we were here in this courtroom, listening to the judge actually say it stunned me. Sure, Daniel believed he had enough evidence to arrest Zach, but what seemed lacking was a motive. Zach didn't know Mr. Schwartz any better than I, so why would he want to kill him? I could easily bring to mind others who might have wanted the man dead.

Wondering about this, I zoned out the legalese going on in front of me. Some phrases penetrated my consciousness like "no previous convictions" and "not a flight risk," and I glanced at Daniel, waiting for him to dispute that and mention the tickets purchased to fly to Toronto. For whatever reason, maybe in deference to me, he didn't bring it up.

For someone like me, obsessed with TV courtroom dramas and crime shows, it was strange that I couldn't seem to focus on the proceedings. At this moment, only one thing mattered: getting Zach out of here. I jumped at the banging of the judge's gavel. "Pay the bailiff," he commanded. At that, I stood and started forward, not sure from the guards flanking the bench, which one was the bailiff.

David Bernstein approached me. "Miss Fine?" The styling of his serge suit screamed "custom-tailored." The lawyer didn't appear much older than me. This baby-faced young man was Mr. Schwartz's longtime attorney?

"Yes. I'm Trudie Fine. Mr. Bernstein?"

He held out his hand. "Alan. Alan Bernstein, David's son. My father couldn't make it on such short notice, so he sent me. I'm a junior associate at the firm." Dark lashes fringed his golden eyes.

I shook his hand. "Thank you for your help today, Mr. Bernstein."

"Alan."

"Alan, how much do I owe you?" I pulled out my checkbook and held my breath.

"Not a thing. Mrs. Schwartz covered all costs. She's posting bond as well. I'll make a quick visit to the bailiff over there, and Mr. Cohen is free to go."

"Posting his bond, too?" I tried not to show my relief. I would have to visit Mrs. Schwartz later to thank her. I'd been meaning to talk to her anyway to find out what she was trying to tell me the day of the funeral. I just hoped she'd be sober.

"Well, thank you again, Mr. Bern...I mean Alan."

"Any time, Miss Fine."

"Trudie."

"Trudie. Here's my card if I can be of help in the future," he said with a quick wink before he turned to pay the bailiff.

Daniel joined me, careful not to make any bodily contact. After all, he had been the arresting officer, and I was the defendant's friend. He also knew I wanted to keep our relationship a secret from Zach.

"Daniel, I have to talk to you."

His cell phone rang, and he held up his hand. "Yeah?" he said into the phone.

"Oh yeah? I'll be right there." He hung the phone on his belt. "Gotta go."

"But, I have to...."

"Sorry, Trudie. I'll call you later, okay?" Daniel headed down the aisle and out the double doors.

"But...." My voice trailed off as the doors swung shut behind him.

A minute later, Zach walked toward me, first tentative, then faster. I caught him in my arms and held him tightly. "Zach. Thank goodness."

We grinned at each other. Then I grabbed his hand and headed for the door. "C'mon. Let's get the halibut out of here."

As I drove to the warehouse, Zach and I kept sneaking peeks at each other and laughing out loud. Color was already returning to his face as we grinned nonstop.

Now, talking about the huge loss of supplies, we both attempted to look grave, but again broke out in smiles. I was glad he'd already seen the damage in the office and warehouse the day before, so I wouldn't have to prepare him. It didn't matter that we faced several days of work getting our office and warehouse back in shape. I'd brought a change of clothes with me, and we were ready to roll up our sleeves and dig in. Zach was free, and that was the only thing that mattered right now.

But when we arrived at the warehouse, I stopped the car right in the middle of the lot.

"What—?" I couldn't finish my question.

Parked in front of our building were several vehicles—cars, SUVs, trucks. I double-parked, blocking a pick-up that sat in front our office entrance, flung open my door and sprang from the car. In an instant, Zach was beside me. The overhead garage door stood open and people bustled around inside.

Zach and I approached the entrance, wide-eyed and speechless.

Not only had the glass been completely swept from the floor, the metal shelves had all been righted and stood half filled with new dishes and glassware.

"Hey, shuga. Hey, Zach." May came over and put her arms around us both in a group hug.

"Wh—what's all this?" I clung to her thin frame as if she were a life preserver.

"I told ya' we were goin' to help, so here we are. Ain't nothin' goin' on come Monday, caterin'-wise. Everyone was available."

She swept her arm out, releasing us, and we stood back to survey the unreality of it all. "You know Johnny, don't ya'?" May asked. "We spoke about him last night."

A lanky man with skin the color of dusty mahogany nodded our way and tipped his hat.

"And this is Michelle Dupree from The Creperie and Andrew Wong, who has the Only Dim Sum food truck in Chinatown."

They both waved and then went back to stacking plates on the shelving units.

"We brought our extra supplies—labeled the shelves so ya'd know where to return them once y'all are back on your feet."

Tears stung my eyes, and I swallowed the lump that had formed. I hurled myself at May, almost knocking her over. "I know you talked about helping us, but I never thought it would be this soon—or this much." I stood back and regarded the others. "Thank you all so much. I don't know how I can ever repay you for this."

"Shuga, you can repay us simply by helping out when one of us is in trouble. And you know that's gonna happen." They all chuckled and nodded in agreement.

"Of course we will."

Zach stood motionless. I had forgotten to tell him about May's offer to help. This was a complete shock to him. He inched his way into the warehouse and walked along the shelving units stocked with supplies, running his fingertips along plates and pots and stemware. Then he turned to face everyone, his eyes and cheeks shining. "I have no words. Just—thank you."

"Check out the office," May said, nodding in that direction.

"You're kidding." I took Zach's hand, and we headed up the four steps into the office.

Perfectly clean. Tables and chairs and filing cabinets all back in place, police dust cleaned away. I opened my desk drawers. Neater than I'd left them. Files in the cabinets back in alpha order. Between the office and the warehouse, I'd expected a good week of cleaning for Zach and me. Instead, we were literally back in business.

I picked up the phone. "All of you must be starving after working here all morning. I'm going to order some pizza. While we're waiting, Zach and I will help out in the warehouse. It's the least we can do."

"No you will not." May held up her hand. "We're almost finished and Johnny's already got some o' his delicious barbequed ribs smokin' away nice and slow for us back at his place. Wanna join us?"

"It's tempting, but we've got lots to do this afternoon."

"Then you two get yo'selves off somewhere and put some decent food into this young man's stomach. Nothin' for you to do here."

Zach and I stopped to eat lunch at a new place that served wood-fired pizza. I ordered a large pie with basil, pine nuts and gorgonzola, then smiled as he devoured three huge pieces.

"Outstanding," Zach pronounced after his first bite. "You should have seen what they called food in that place. God, I hope that lawyer can get me off. No way I want to spend any more time in jail."

"Don't worry. They're going to catch the real killer soon."

"How do you know? Any ideas who it could be?" Zach's eyebrows knitted together.

"I've been doing a little sleuthing, and I see a few possible suspects. I've told Dan—I mean, Detective Goldman—about them, too. So I know he's following up on my leads."

"What leads?"

I paused. "Zach, I'm not going to tell you who or why these people are suspects. I think it's better for you not to know. That way, you can answer any questions with total honesty." I put my hand over his. "Just let me handle this. Okay?"

Zach turned his hand palm up and grasped mine. "Trudie, don't get in over your head with this. Don't forget what someone did to our business—and to you. It might have been a warning."

His eyes shone with concern, and his hold on my hand lingered. We exchanged a quick glance, and I knew he was thinking about his declaration of love for me yesterday in the car.

I gently slipped my hand out of his grasp. "Don't worry. My plan is to pass any information I have to Goldman. Then he can handle it. I'll be fine."

I wasn't going to tell Zach about the threatening phone call I received in the middle of the night. He had enough on his mind.

# Chapter Nineteen

I dropped Zach at his apartment, and headed off to see Mrs. Schwartz. After all, she had not only covered the attorney's fees; she had paid the bail money to free Zach. I wasn't sure why she'd been so generous, but I needed to thank her. I also hoped she could provide more clues as to who might have murdered her husband.

Graciella greeted me at the door and led me to the patio off the kitchen where Mrs. Schwartz lounged in a white tank top and shorts, which showed off her burnished skin. She wore sunglasses, and spikes of platinum hair stuck out the top of her pink sun visor. She held a drink in one hand, and a cigarette poked out between two extended fingers.

"Trudie, how nice to see you." She put down her cigarette and drink and held out both hands to me. I bent to kiss her cheek. "Please sit down. Graciella, some iced tea, please, for our guest."

I still wore my purple power suit from the morning's proceedings.

I took off the jacket and laid it across the back of my lounge chair. Then I slipped off my sandals, put my feet up, and sighed. I hadn't realized how frenzied my life had become until I actually had a moment to relax.

"How are you doing, Mrs. Schwartz?" I couldn't believe it had only been a little over a week since her husband's murder. So much had happened.

She nodded slightly and smiled at me. "I'm—getting along. It's going to take some time. So, tell me. How did the hearing go this morning?" She sipped her drink, a watered down iced tea; watered down with vodka, most likely.

Graciella placed my tea on a side table, and I took a big gulp before responding. "Everything went great. Mr. Bernstein's son handled it well, and Zach is free, for now. Mrs. Schwartz, I must thank you for all you did for Zach—paying the attorney's fee and the bail money. That was much too generous."

"No need to thank me, dear. I feel utterly responsible for his arrest."

"Responsible? Why?"

"Well, if the two of you hadn't been catering our party, Zachary never would have been arrested. Why the police would suspect such a nice boy of Melvin's m-m-murd…, well you know, I just can't conceive. He hardly knew the man. For my part, I know for sure that he is not to blame."

"Mrs. Schwartz, the day you sat Shiva, you tried to tell me something, but you were too—upset." Limp as an overcooked noodle and passed out on the sofa was more like it. "I'm sure it was important. Maybe something you saw or heard. I don't know what it was, but you indicated that you wanted me to know about it."

She took a sip of her drink and was silent for a few moments stared straight ahead toward the pool. At least the police tape had been removed, returning the patio and pool deck back to normal.

I wondered if she'd heard what I'd said.

She put down her drink and turned to me. "I think it has something to do with the brother."

"The brother? Mr. Schwartz's brother?"

She shook her head. "No. Allison's brother."

"But Ally doesn't have a brother."

"Trudie, you know Allison is adopted, don't you?"

"Yes, of course. Her mother and father were just teens. So you and Mr. Schwartz adopted her."

"Yes, that's right. But evidently, Allison's birth father later married another woman and had a son."

"So Ally has a half-brother." I wondered where Mrs. Schwartz was going with this. "She never mentioned him."

"She didn't know about him until maybe a year ago. First, he wrote her a letter telling her that they had the same father, that he was her half-brother. Then, he called her to introduce himself. He was very personable, and Allison asked if he wanted to meet in person."

"Did they? Meet, I mean."

"No. Every time they picked a place and time, he didn't show up.

But the phone calls continued. Allison's restaurant was doing well at the time, and she was very busy. He told her to think of him as her brother. He was happy about her success and would always be there for her. That was about the time Allison got bored with all the paperwork involved with running a restaurant, and hired a general manager, got a little too close with him, if you know what I mean. And you know how that ended up." She raised her eyebrows at me expectantly.

"He ran off with the profits. I remember."

She nodded. "That's right."

"Well," she continued. "I'd never seen Allison's father so angry. Melvin was upset with her for allowing it to happen, for turning her back on the business after he had invested several hundred thousand dollars. She was so self-involved that she lost the restaurant."

Mrs. Schwartz lit another cigarette, took a drag and exhaled a long stream of smoke. "She begged Melvin to save the restaurant for her, but he wouldn't do it. Insisted she needed to learn her lesson. If she wanted to be a restaurateur, then she would have to take full responsibility for its success—or failure." Mrs. Schwartz shook her head. "It was awful. Allison didn't speak to her father for months."

"What does any of this have to do with her half-brother?" I asked.

"After her general manager disappeared, the brother called her. He said that he was going to make that guy pay for what he did." Mrs. Schwartz shifted her body toward me and had to catch herself from falling off the lounge. "Allison said he sounded kind of scary. She told him over and over to let the police handle it. But he insisted he was her brother and he would take care of it."

The more Mrs. Schwartz talked about this unknown brother of Ally's, the more I had the sensation that I'd left something burning in the oven. "What's his name?"

"His name...let's see." She stretched out on the lounge chair, a slight grin on her face. From the side, I could see behind her sunglass lens that she had closed her eyes.

Uh, oh. I was losing her again. "Mrs. Schwartz?"

She turned her head to me and lifted her sunglasses, opening one eye. "Why Trudie. How nice to see you, dear."

"You were about to tell me Allison's brother's name."

"Oh yes. Steven. That's it. Thteven."

"Do you know his last name?"

"Of course. It was a private adopsun. We paid all of the mother's hosp'al bills. Allison's birth father came to see her at the hospital the day we picked her up. Ohh, little Allithon was such a cutie, li'l blonde withps."

Mrs. Schwartz began to tear up, her speech slurring more and more, and I was afraid I would lose her before she gave me all the information I needed. She picked up her napkin and blew her nose then pulled down her sunglasses and lay back in her chair.

"Mrs. Schwartz, the birth father's last name. What was it?"

"Hith last name wath...Carter? Carson? No, it was Carver. Definitely Carver."

"So her brother's name is Steven Carver," I thought out loud. Some piece was missing. I knew I was getting close but just couldn't get there, like trying to light the grill over and over, but it just won't ignite.

I swung my legs over the side of the lounge chair and leaned toward her. "Mrs. Schwartz, please don't think I'm being disrespectful, but do you have any idea who might have killed your husband?"

Lifting her sunglasses and perching them atop her sun visor among the platinum spikes, she turned to peer at me. "I'm not exackly sure," she said, her speech thick as maple syrup. "But Trudie, dear, you are a thmart girl. You and Ally put your heads togetter, and I know you'll figger it out." Then she pulled the glasses down over her eyes and slumped back into her chair.

She was right. The only person who could tell me more was Ally. I thanked Mrs. Schwartz again, though she didn't seem to notice, and drove to Ally's condo. I had some tough questions for her and wondered whether she'd be willing to give me some straight answers.

"OH, IT'S YOU." Ally peered through her partially opened door. She looked very young, her face clean and freckled without makeup and her blonde hair pulled back into a ponytail.

"Can I come in for a few minutes? I'd like to thank you for getting that lawyer for Zach." I spoke in calm, gentle tones as if I were poaching eggs, easing them into simmering water so the yolks wouldn't break.

She hesitated. "I guess so." She turned and walked into her living room, leaving me on my own to follow her into the apartment and close the door.

Ally stretched herself out on her sofa with her bare feet propped up and her arms crossed as if to say, "Go ahead."

"I don't know how to thank you. The lawyer worked his magic, and with your mom's financial help, Zach is free on bond."

"Thank my mother for that, not me." She wasn't going to give me an inch.

"I did. I was just over there thanking her. But you're the one who arranged for the lawyer, and I'm sure you were the one who asked your mother to post bail money for Zach."

"Contrary to what you think, Trudie, I do care about Zach. He's always been there for me." Her stare was intense and defied me to make any snide remarks about some of the trouble she'd gotten herself into.

I cleared my throat. "Ally." I paused, trying to choose my words carefully. "Listen, I'm sorry I came on so strong the other day. I'm not blaming you for your father's death. But we both know Zach didn't kill him. So maybe if we put together everything we know we can figure out who the real murderer is. Can I ask you a few questions?"

"About what? You think I had something to do with it, don't you?" She chewed on her bottom lip.

"No, I don't believe that." It occurred to me then that, although I'd had questions about the cookie bars she'd made for Mr. Schwartz and about her relationship with Mr. Lewis, I really didn't think Ally was capable of killing her own father, the man who had doted on her all her life, even if he hadn't rescued her restaurant. "But I think you may have information that could lead us to the killer."

"You think I'm hiding something?"

"I think you don't realize that some things you know would be very helpful to solve this case—and might prevent another murder." This time I was thinking of myself and my brush with doom the day before.

"Another murder? Whose? And what information could I possibly have?" She uncrossed her arms and held them up in a questioning manner.

"I—saw you yesterday, at the Hilton in Bethesda," I hedged, ignoring her questions.

Her head jerked up. "And?"

"Why were you meeting Mr. Lewis at a hotel? What's going on between you two?"

Ally put her head back and laughed. Then her eyes widened. "You think I'm having an affair with Mr. Lewis? You've got to be kidding. He's old enough to be my father."

"Why else were you meeting him in a hotel room of all places?"

"Why not meet him in a hotel room? My tennis lesson was just down the street from there, and I needed to talk to Bob in private."

"Bob, is it?" I lifted my eyebrows.

"Yes, that's what I've always called him. He was Daddy's partner, for God's sake. And a good friend of the family who I've known my whole life."

"Why were you meeting him in private?" I persisted.

"I'd been speaking with him for a couple of months about funding a restaurant for me. I had a new concept that I didn't want overheard by big ears in a restaurant."

"Why not meet him here in your condo?"

"And have his wife find out and think we were having an affair?" She rolled her eyes at me.

"What would she think if she found out you were meeting in a hotel?" I rolled my eyes right back at her. "I'm not a detective, but if I was able to discover your secret meeting, Mrs. Lewis, or any PI she hired, certainly could have as well."

"You think she hired a private investigator to follow her husband?"

"I have no idea. I'm just saying—oh, never mind. So you're telling me that your rendezvous with Mr. Lewis in a hotel was a purely innocent meeting about him backing your new restaurant concept?"

"Exactly."

I released my breath in a frustrated sigh and folded my hands in my lap. "Okay. New subject. Why did you book airline tickets for you and Zach to Toronto? That was the reason the police thought he was a flight risk and arrested him."

"Airline tickets to Toronto? I didn't book any tickets to Toronto." She shook her head, her lips parted in surprise.

"Yes, you did. The reservations were copied to Zach's email, and they came from you," I insisted. "They were charged to your American Express account."

"I didn't make any plane reservations. Why would I want to go to

Toronto?" Her quizzical expression was convincing.

"To run away with Zach."

Ally's mouth was open again, and she shook her head as if I was nutty as an ice cream sundae.

"Well, someone made airline reservations for you and Zach," I said. "And they did it from your computer; well, at least, from your email address." For the first time, I wondered if someone was trying to frame Ally. Or Zach.

Ally held up her hands and shrugged. Then she frowned. "Could someone be using my email account? Oh my God, and my credit card?" She stood up and began pacing. She didn't know a thing about these airline tickets, I realized.

"It sounds like it," I said. "You'd better check your statement. And call your credit card company to reverse the charge and cancel the account. I'd probably change my email address, too, if I were you."

Ally smiled at me and shook her head.

"What?" I asked.

"I miss you, Trudie. You always knew what to do when I had a problem. When you were around, life seemed so much simpler. I could always rely on you for good advice. Whatever happened to our friendship?"

"I don't know. I guess we both got busy with our careers."

"Do you think...?" She gazed at me shyly. "Could we be friends again?"

I thought about this. Ally and I did have a good relationship as college roommates.

"I was always envious of you, Trudie."

"Envious of me? Why? You're gorgeous and thin and wealthy. What more could someone want?" I asked.

"But you were the one with all the friends. Everyone at school liked you. You had this passion…about cooking. I would have loved to be passionate about something, anything. Even owning my own restaurant, something I'd always wanted, became tedious. It was never enough for me."

She dipped her head and I could see tears in her eyes. "Daddy was right, you know. Not to bail me out. Oh, I raved and carried on and we didn't speak for months. But he did the right thing. I needed a wake-up call."

I smiled at her. "Yeah. It probably was the best thing he could have done for you."

Suddenly, her face lit up. "Trudie, I have this great concept for a restaurant. Not one, but a chain of restaurants with delicious food that is healthy. But we won't advertise it that way. People think healthy food means tofu and steamed vegetables."

Ally stood up and started pacing again, but this time with nervous excitement. "Bob is going to help me get up and running. We'll have menu items like Unfried Chicken and Spicy Baked Fries and Maltless Shakes. Everything will taste yummy, but without all the fat and sugar and white flour." She turned to me with a huge smile, and her face radiated joy.

Propelled by her enthusiasm, I got up and hugged her. "I think you're going to be all right, Ally. I'm so happy for you."

"Do you think we can be friends again?" she asked.

I grinned at her. "Only if you'll let me finish asking you these questions."

She sat back down. "I'm listening."

"Okay," I continued. "So you're not having an affair with Mr. Lewis."

"No," she giggled.

"And you didn't make airline reservations for you and Zach to run off to Toronto."

"No," she said in a loud, emphatic tone.

"All right then. One more thing and then I'm done. Tell me about your brother. Your mom told me you have a half-brother."

"Steven? There's nothing to tell really. He first contacted me about a year ago. I had no idea I had a brother. Even though we'd never met in person, he insisted he cared about me. Kept calling me saying that siblings needed to stick together and that he had my back. Kinda weird." She shook her head and shrugged.

"Did Steven know what happened with your restaurant? I mean, why it folded?"

"Yes. He'd been calling me on and off, and I started to confide in him. Steven was the only person who would listen to me, hear my side of the story."

"So he knew about the general manager who took the money and ran?"

"Yes, he knew about him. He kept insisting that he would take care of the guy himself. Steven sounded kind of creepy, so I told him to let the police handle it."

"Did Steven also know that your father wouldn't give you the money to keep the restaurant open?"

"Oh, yeah. I was so pissed with Daddy, and Steven would call and I'd scream and cry and carry on. He tried to console me, telling me that all fathers were nasty bastards who didn't care about their kids. We kind of fed into each other's misery."

"So Steven had a problem with his father, too?"

"Well, yes. His father cheated with other women. Made his mom miserable."

Something kept gnawing at me, but I just couldn't figure out what.

"Have we finished the interrogation?" Ally asked.

"I guess so," I said, more puzzled than ever.

"Are we good now?" she asked, smiling.

I smiled back. Maybe I'd been too hard on Ally lately. "We're good," I nodded.

I started for the door and then turned.

"Just one more question."

Ally groaned.

"Whatever happened to that general manager—the one who ran off with all the money?" I'd been curious about that for some time. "Did he get away scot free?"

"Oh, they found him, all right. He'd taken another job as general manager of a restaurant in Chicago. Changed his name, cut all ties with friends and associates."

"Did they arrest him?"

Ally frowned. "They discovered his body, frozen in the restaurant walk-in cooler."

"The walk-in cooler?"

"Yes, they called it an accident, but I figured a guy that crooked has plenty of enemies. He probably tried to steal from them, too. In the back of my mind, though, I kept wondering about Steven who always talked about getting even. I mean, he's a little weird, but do you think he would do something like that? Just because he's my half-brother?"

A tingle crept up my spine, and I shivered. In fact, I couldn't stop shivering.

"Trudie, are you all right?" Ally asked.

"I-I-m f-f-fine," I lied.

She walked me to the sofa, sat me down and covered me with the creamsicle-colored fleece throw that had been draped across the arm. Then she opened a cabinet and poured an amber-colored liquid into a small glass. "Here, Trudie. Drink this."

I scrutinized the glass, doubtful about its contents.

"It's just brandy. Go ahead. I guarantee it will help."

The first sip gave me a jolt. But as the liquid moved through my system, it warmed me. I took another sip, and another. Ally was right. It did make me feel better. Soon the shivers were gone, and my nerves were as calm as butter cream icing smoothed across the top of a cake.

"Are you okay now?"

"Yes, a little better. Ally?"

"What?"

"Yesterday, at my warehouse—"

"Uh-huh."

"Someone locked me in the walk-in cooler."

# Chapter Twenty

On the way home, I kept peering into my rearview mirror, checking to see if I was being followed. I dialed and redialed Daniel's number, but got his voice mail every time. I left three messages for him to call me. Had he already gotten tired of me or, like a typical guy, panicked that he was getting too close? Or maybe after all these years I was just paranoid about men.

All of a sudden, home didn't seem like the place I wanted to be. I didn't want to pull into the parking garage or go up to my apartment alone. Daniel wasn't there to escort me safely into my apartment or check for intruders. Even if I did get home safely, would I be harassed by threatening phone calls again? My body began to shake so much I could have blended a daiquiri.

I turned the car around and headed to the only place where I knew I would feel safe: my parents' house. There my mother would make me her special blueberry pancakes and hot cocoa. I could sleep the entire night without worry, bundled beneath my purple comforter and cuddled with my white stuffed childhood friend, Hopper, the bunny. I'd sleep in an old oversized t-shirt from my high school days. I even kept a toothbrush there for occasions like this.

What was I thinking? There were never occasions like this.

I knew that nothing bad could happen on this quaint, tree-lined street in Bethesda where I'd grown up, the houses populated by empty-nesters and young families. But when I pulled up to the curb at my parents' house, their car was gone. Darn! Where the hamburger were they? But, okay. This would still be a safe haven until I could get in touch with Daniel. I gathered my purse and jacket from the passenger seat and opened the car door.

"Well hello, Trudie. Fancy meeting you here."

I jumped and turned, banging my knee on the steering wheel.

Holding my car door open, and smiling brightly, was none other than Bradley Miller.

My heart vaulted to my throat.

He put his hand on my shoulder. "I'm sorry. I startled you, didn't I?"

"Well, yes. I didn't expect anyone to be standing here when I opened the car door." The brandy Ally had given me must have worn off because I began to shiver again.

Bradley stopped smiling, and his forehead creased in concern. His hand, still resting on my shoulder, felt clammy as it moved down my arm. "Trudie, you're trembling. Are you okay?" His eyes, which had darkened to a forest green, bored into mine.

"I'm fine. But what are you doing here?" Just a couple of days ago, I would have melted like a pat of butter in a frying pan with Bradley standing so close, touching me. Today, I wanted to run and hide.

He put both hands on the roof of the car and leaned toward me. "I wanted to thank your parents for that great dinner last night. I brought flowers for your mom." He gestured toward the house and shook his head. "But I guess they're not home."

I gathered my purse, jacket and keys and turned to signal him that I wanted to get out of the car. "Just give the flowers to me, and I'll let them know you stopped by."

Bradley didn't move. For the first time, I noticed his appearance. He sported the same preppy clothes he wore yesterday—a horizontal striped polo and khakis, but the shirt was only half-tucked into his wrinkled slacks. The streaked blond hair I'd admired before now appeared jaundiced in the sunlight and damp from perspiration.

"I think I'll just wait for them," he said. "Shall we wait together?"

"Listen, Bradley. It was thoughtful of you to stop by and bring flowers for Mom. She'll be delighted. But I've had a long day and didn't get much sleep last night. I just want to go inside. Okay?"

"Sure. How did Zach's hearing go this morning?"

"It went well. He's free for now and hopefully forever if the police catch the real killer. So if you'll just let me out of my car..." What was it going to take to get Bradley to leave?

"Oh." He shifted his body sideways, barely leaving room for me to slip by him and close the car door. Was he clueless or what? Why hadn't I seen this side of him before? Sweat beaded on his upper lip.

Finally, after an awkward pause, he walked to his car, extracted a bouquet of red roses and handed them to me as if he was cradling a whole red snapper in his arms.

I managed a smile. "Thanks. I'll be sure to let Mom know these are from you."

He stood still like a lost boy. "You'll call me if you need my help, right?"

"I've got your number." I knew I would need help at the vodka and caviar event at the law firm on Wednesday, but maybe I would call the bartender agency instead. I didn't think I could deal with Bradley any more. He was too intense. I just wanted some anonymous guy to come, do the job, and leave—no strings attached.

I waited until Bradley drove away and then entered my parents' house. All I wanted to do was climb into my old bed and take a nice long nap.

IT WAS SO cold. Men's suits and jackets and trousers hung stiff as cutting boards. I spotted rows of sweaters neatly folded on shelves, but when I picked one up, it cracked into shards of ice and fell to the floor. I shivered in my thin t-shirt, my bare feet sliding along slick ice as I headed for the closed door. The knob was encrusted with ice, and I couldn't get a good enough grip to turn it. I began to pound on the door with both hands, but my palms stuck to the frozen metal and wouldn't pull away.

"Help. Open the door. Get me out of here," I rasped, but my

vocal chords had freeze-dried, and only puffs of frosty mist emerged from my mouth into the air.

"Trudie. Trudie, wake up."

My shoulders were shaking.

"Wha—what?" I opened my eyes.

My mother sat on the bed leaning over me, her hands on my shoulders. "You were having a bad dream, honey."

"I was?" My body trembled.

Frowning, my mother covered me with the blanket and comforter and then sat down next to me on the bed. She put a hand to my forehead. "Poor baby. Are you all right?"

"I am now. Just a bad dream. Where were you?"

"Daddy and I went to a matinee at the Regal. The prices are much lower on a weekday afternoon. And with the senior discount and our theater club card points, they practically pay us to come watch movies." She reached over and smoothed the hair out of my eyes.

"Well, I'm glad you're home." I sat up and hugged my knees.

I relaxed in the normalcy of my old bedroom, my mother sporting one of her typical pants outfits, this one a mint green. Her smile glowed, but creases around her eyes and lips showed concern.

"What are you doing here? Not that I'm upset that my daughter chose to make an unexpected visit."

I sighed. "I've had a rough week."

A frown shadowed her face. "What's wrong?"

"What's wrong? Mr. Schwartz's murder, my business ransacked, Zach's arrest, not to mention my parents embarrassing me to death at dinner last night."

"Trudie, we were just being sociable. After all, how many times does our daughter bring home eligible young men, much less three of them at the same time? Bradley and Daniel were perfectly fine with the conversation and, obviously, both enamored with you."

"Well I wasn't fine with it. Anyway, did you see the flowers in the foyer? Bradley brought them by to thank you for dinner last night."

Mom's eyes lit up. "How thoughtful. He really is a very charming young man, Trudie."

"He has his moments." I understood my mother's reaction to him. He'd had me under his spell the last week. But now I had my doubts about Bradley, but I couldn't pinpoint exactly what they were.

"Anyway," I continued, softening my tone. "You and Dad need to back off a little. I've only known them for a week. Let's take it a step at a time, okay?"

She brushed my bangs back out of my eyes and smiled. "Okay, honey. I promise to be good next time. I'll speak to your dad, too."

I brightened. "Zach's been released on bail. So maybe we can get back to work and back to normal."

"That's wonderful news. Things will get better now. I'm sure the police will catch the real murderer. That nice Detective Goldman will solve the crime."

I smiled. Yes, that nice Detective Goldman would solve the case. My stomach growled. "What time is it?"

"Five-thirty. Are you hungry?"

"Famished."

"Good." She stood up. "How about some nice chicken and dumplings?"

"Comfort food. Perfect. Thanks, Mom."

She knelt and kissed me on the forehead.

As she headed out the door, I called after her. "Tell me now why I moved out into my own place?"

I reached over to the nightstand where I'd left my cell phone, sunk back into the pillows and dialed Daniel.

"Trudie. Where have you been? I've been trying to reach you." I heard the alarm in Daniel's voice.

"You've been trying to reach me? I left you at least three messages asking you to call me right away. I've needed to talk to you all day. Where have you been?"

"I'm in the middle of an investigation. Involved in some heavy surveillance. But when I returned your call, you didn't answer. I went to your apartment, banged on your door. I was so worried, I got the super to let me in. Where are you?"

"Really? You were that worried about me?" My heart fluttered. Never in my entire life had a guy actually worried about me. Except maybe Zach. But he was my best friend so that didn't count.

"Of course I was worried. I heard your messages. What's going on? Where are you?"

"I'm at my parents' house. My phone must have been on vibrate. Sorry."

I had so much to tell Daniel I didn't know where to begin. I had to tell him about the threatening phone call during the night and my conversations with Mrs. Schwartz and Ally, about the half-brother and the tickets to Toronto and Ally's relationship with Bob Lewis.

And this weird feeling about Bradley.

"Daniel, so much has happened. I'm having dinner here with my parents. Can you meet me at my apartment about eight o'clock? In the parking garage so you can walk me upstairs. Okay?"

"Trudie, of course I'll meet you at your place, but what's going on? You need to tell me now."

I hesitated. Maybe I should tell him at least the most important information, like the scary phone call and Ally's half-brother. But Mom was calling me to dinner. "A couple of hours won't make a difference. There's just too much to tell. Can't we do this later, in person?"

"Sure. We have all night. I'm not going anywhere."

I closed my eyes and exhaled the breath I didn't realize I'd been holding. Daniel was going to stay with me tonight. That was exactly what I needed.

# Chapter Twenty-One

The drive home was thankfully uneventful. At seven-thirty on a July evening, the sun, although beginning to set, still brightened the sky. Mom's chicken and dumplings had warmed my belly and satisfied my soul.

I pulled into my parking garage at seven-fifty, turned off the ignition, and waited for Daniel. And waited. Eight o'clock came and went. Eight ten. Eight fifteen. I called his cell phone. No answer. Where was he?

As it got later, I began to feel uncomfortable sitting in my car in the garage. I might as well go up to my apartment while other people were coming and going and before the darkness cast shadows in every corner. No danger lurking right now. I called Daniel's number again and left him a message. "I'm headed upstairs, unescorted. But I can't wait to see you. Come soon," I whispered into the phone in a breathy hiss, trying to sound sexy. I wanted my voice to sizzle like pepper steak with rice when it hits a steaming hot platter at Mr. Wu's.

A couple I recognized approached the entrance. I got out of my car, locked it, and followed them into the building. When the elevator reached my floor, I was alone. I checked the hallway. No one in sight. I hurried down the hall, entered my condo, slammed the door shut and locked it. Then I leaned back against the door, breathing hard.

Made it. But had I, really? Daniel wasn't here this time to check each room for unwanted guests. Slowly, I began to survey the apartment. The living room appeared fine; no one behind the sofa. My small galley kitchen was also clear. I took off my sandals and padded slowly toward the bathroom. I swung the door inward so it tapped the wall and inched my way into the room. The shower curtain could easily conceal someone. Holding my breath, I grabbed the edge and, like pulling off a band-aid to lessen the pain, yanked it back. Empty. I released my breath.

My hands trembled as I approached my bedroom. There were so many places to hide in a bedroom—in the closet, on the floor behind the bed, under the bed, behind the door. Did I really want to go into the bedroom? What would I do if I found someone there? I hoped I'd be fast enough to get out the door. But I'd locked the deadbolt, which would slow me down. Maybe I should unlock it for a quick escape. Or maybe I would just wait in the living room until Daniel arrived.

Where was Daniel?

A knock on the door made me jump.

"Daniel," I whispered with relief and ran to the door. Fumbling with the lock, I finally swung the door wide.

"Hi, Trudie." Bradley stood grinning at me. "Can I come in?"

I froze, mouth open. Before I could say a word, he pushed the door wider with one hand, strode in, and slammed the door shut behind him.

"Actually," I sputtered. "I'm expecting someone. Any minute."

"Oh yeah? Who?" He sauntered over to the sofa and sat down, crossing his legs. He wore scuffed cordovan penny loafers and no socks.

"Detective Goldman. We have some things to discuss. Privately."

"I'm sure you two have lots to discuss privately. Ha!" His laugh sounded humorless.

Something was out of kilter. Here, like at my parents' house earlier, this wasn't the Bradley I knew. I'd never seen him anything but friendly and helpful. He scared me a little.

Sitting down on the opposite end of the sofa, I decided to try a different approach. "Bradley, Mom was thrilled with your roses. She put them in her favorite Waterford crystal vase on the table in the foyer. It was thoughtful of you."

"I like your mother. She's a great cook—like you."

"I'll take that as a compliment." Maybe my strategy of keeping him calm with normal conversation was working. "Is there something you want to talk to me about?"

"You're damn right there's something I want to talk about."

I stood up. Something definitely wasn't right. "Uh—could I get you a cold drink? It's pretty hot out. You must be thirsty." If I could just get into the kitchen, I could call 9-1-1 and leave the phone off the hook. Or I could grab a knife to defend myself, if necessary.

"No. I'm here to talk. To you. Sit down." He nodded to the sofa where I'd just been sitting.

"I'm fine standing."

"I said to sit down." He stood, grabbed my arm and threw me onto the couch.

"Bradley. What in the world has gotten into you?" Half sitting, half lying across the cushions, I struggled to straighten myself out.

"Let's talk, Trudie." He stood over me. He was frowning and intense. Upset.

"Talk about what?" The back of my neck and scalp prickled as if each hair stood at attention.

"You need to stop badgering her. Stop making her sad." His face was almost pouty, like a little boy's.

"Badgering who? My mom?"

"No. Allison. You went to see her today and made her sad." How did Bradley know I'd gone to see Ally?

"Yes, I did see her today. But we had a good talk and made up. We're friends. She was fine when I left her. Really."

"Fine. You call that fine?" Bradley began to pace, his hands gesturing with every word. "She called me this afternoon to question my motives. She asked if I knew what happened to that scumbag manager who screwed her out of everything. Even accused me of using her credit card and booking airline tickets for her and Zach."

Then he turned to face me, his face reddening like a boiled crab. He pointed his finger at me. "What did you say to her? What did you tell her?"

"Wha—? I don't understand. Bradley, why would Ally call you?

She doesn't even know y—."

Oh, my God. Of course; I understood now. It hit me like a Hawaiian Punch. Bradley was Ally's half-brother, Steven. She'd never met him in person so she wouldn't have recognized him the night of the murder or at the funeral or the Shiva house. But there he'd been at every step of the way. Most likely, he'd been following Ally for the past year, watching her every move and then finding out everything else from their phone conversations. I examined him more closely now, and there it had been right in front of me all along. His eyes, the shape of his face, the dimples—he could have been her twin. Why had I never noticed the resemblance?

I held out my hand to him, pointing. "You're—Steven. Ally's brother."

He gave a brisk nod. "Damn straight. And I don't like the way you've been treating her, accusing her of things she's never done. I heard the way you spoke to her in that bar, Trudie. You threatened her about going to the police. Poor Allison was scared to death. You scared her."

"You were there? At the bar?"

"Of course I was there. How else could I protect my sister? Someone has to have her back."

I swallowed hard and tried to keep my voice from quivering. "Bradley—I mean Steven—please sit down and let's discuss this. It's obviously been bothering you."

He plopped onto the sofa and folded his arms.

"Steven." I kept my voice as quiet and steady as I could. "Ally allowed Zach to be arrested for killing that girl at the University of Maryland when she knew he didn't do it. Why couldn't she have gone to the police instead of letting Zach be the fall guy?"

"Why should she? She didn't put peanuts in those bars. I did. Allison wanted to be with Zach that night. She's always wanted Zach, but all he cared about was that other girl and her peanut allergies. So I took care of it." His grin twisted into an ugly grimace.

"You? You put peanuts in those bars?" I was having trouble catching my breath, and my body began trembling again. "But that was, what, eight years ago? You didn't even know Ally back then."

"Sure I did. She just didn't know me."

He'd been following Ally for years? What else did he do to "protect" his half-sister?

I didn't want to ask the question, but I had to know. "What about the cookie bars Ally made for her father? Did she…?"

"What kind of friend are you? Allison wouldn't do that to her father." He shook his head.

I stared at him, wondering why I hadn't seen through all that charm to the despicable human being who sat in front of me now.

"He had to be punished, don't you see, for what he did to Allison. Or for what he didn't do. All he had to do to make her happy was to save her restaurant. He had plenty of money—there was no end to his money."

He chuckled again. "Allison actually made it pretty easy for me, delivering her dessert bars to the house. All I had to do was sprinkle the bars generously with peanut dust. Zach had some guy at the party deliver them right to the old man for me. I found Schwartz in the cabana watching some game on TV. He was so delighted that his little girl had made him his favorite treats. Gobbled down a huge piece."

Steven stood up and paced the room, gesturing with his hands while recalling what had happened.

"It was all so easy. The band was on break, smoking around the other side of the house. Didn't even see me. It was pretty quick, too. The old man started wheezing and clutching his throat. Stumbled out of the cabana toward me. You should've seen his face, all splotched and puffy, his eyes big and wide, questioning why I wasn't helping him. Ha! I told him exactly why." Steven grinned. "What a pleasure to watch that man suffer."

Steven's words swum round and round in my head at a dizzying pace. I didn't want to hear any more, but he continued.

"Fell flat on his face on the concrete. I just stuck out my foot and rolled him into the pool. Voila." Steven brushed his hands together as if he'd just completed an important task. Then he slumped back onto the sofa laughing.

This wasn't a human being. He was a monster. "B-but Mr. Schwartz loved Ally. And she loved him, more than anything. How could you take him away from her?"

Steven stood up, leaned over me and bellowed, "He made my sister sad!" His face was flushed, and his eyes had grown as dark as Greek olives.

Swinging away from me, he began to pace the room, muttering to himself. "Fathers are pieces of garbage. They don't deserve the children who love them. Night after night I waited for my father to come home to us, listening to my mother sobbing in her bed. But no, all he cared about was himself and getting into bed with all those other women. Mama was so beautiful, so serene. She kept telling me one day he'd come to his senses, return home to us and he'd stay with us because we loved him and we were his family and he loved his family."

I scanned the room, searching for some type of weapon. I glanced at the door, wondering if somehow I could get to it before Steven. If I didn't find an escape on my own, he'd never let me out of here alive.

Where was Daniel?

Steven stopped pacing and glared at me, still blabbering. "Mama really believed he'd come home. Ha! Once a piece of shit, always a piece of shit. They're all the same. Every last one of them. And they all deserve the same consequences."

"But..."

"Enough talk. Now I need to deal with you."

I sat up straighter. "Detective Goldman will be here any minute, so I'd suggest you get out of here while you can."

"Detective Goldman is not going anywhere," he spat at me.

Suddenly, the air became very thin, and I found it difficult to inhale a full breath. My words caught in my throat. "What did you do to him?"

"Your precious Daniel won't be coming to the rescue tonight.

And we need to finish what we started yesterday. You know—you and the walk-in cooler?"

He paused to let this sink in and then continued. "The thing was I kind of liked you, Trudie. I don't know, I guess I just decided I wanted you around a little longer. So, I let you out." He stepped over to me, leaned down and grasped my chin so I'd look up at him. "You were the only one who understood me. So—I gave you a little more time."

My eyes were wide, locked on his.

"But...all good things have to come to an end. Right? Answer me," he growled, moving my chin up and down to make me nod. "Pretty clever way to get rid of someone, huh? Like the guy in Chicago. He deserved it more than anyone, fucking my sister and then stealing her blind. Oh, excuse me, Trudie. I know you don't like curse words. He filleted her, fantailed her and fried her, and so I fucking froze him like a fish stick." He burst out laughing at his own joke.

My body trembled and an alarm screamed in my head. "What did you do to Daniel?" I shrieked.

Steven chuckled. "I've taken care of all of them now—except you. I warned you about putting your nose where it doesn't belong. I warned you on the phone last night. But still you went ahead anyway, upsetting Allison and her mother about things that don't concern you. Dredging up the past and making my sister sad."

So that explained the threatening call, but what about Daniel? Had Steven really "taken care of him"? Why hadn't I told Daniel everything over the phone? If I'd given him the information I had, he might have put it all together. He might still be alive.

My heart sank.

I'd cared for Daniel. I believed he cared for me. Now he was gone.

And I was next.

# Chapter Twenty-Two

No. I refused to be Steven's next victim. The others had been unsuspecting targets. They had no idea who he was or that he intended to kill them. But I did, and I would get myself out of this. Somehow.

I tried to clear my head and think. It seemed unlikely that Steven had merely pretended to be Bradley over the past week and a half. No one could fake such big differences in their appearance and personality. Could they? Was Bradley actually Steven's alter ego. If that were true, I needed to get Bradley's attention. If I could establish communication with Bradley, I might have a chance.

Steven still paced back and forth murmuring to himself about how and where he would "take care of me." Occasionally, he stopped, contemplated me, and shook his head, then continued pacing.

"Bradley? I'm going to need your help at my next gig on Wednesday. Do you think you'll be available?" I tried to keep my voice from shaking.

His brows lowered. "My name's Steven, not Bradley."

"I'd like to speak to Bradley, please. Is he still there?"

"No, you can't speak to him."

"But I have the perfect job for him. A vodka and caviar event on Wednesday. Zach and I need a good bartender. We need Bradley."

I waited, hopeful that I was right. That Bradley would emerge and save me from certain death.

Steven stopped and faced me. His facial features began to change right in front of me. The furrowed brow smoothed out, the eyes brightened, and the mouth broke into a wide smile.

"Trudie, I would love to help you on Wednesday. But..." He glanced around the room as if fearful of who might be listening. He finished in a whisper. "...I don't think he'll let me."

"Of course he'll let you help. Steven." Addressing the alter ego, I wondered if I was the crazy one now. "Can Bradley work our Wednesday gig?"

Bradley's smile tightened into a frown. He let out a mirthless laugh, bent over me and shook his head. "You are one stupid bitch. There is no Bradley. Only Steven. And, no, I do not have a split personality. I played a great role, don't you think? That's the one thing my father taught me: how to be charming and con everyone around me. But you've run out of luck, lady. Let's go." Steven yanked me up by my arm.

"Go where?" My stomach churned as if filled with popping corn. Did he think he could drag me out of my apartment without drawing attention?

No. I couldn't let this happen. Trudie Fine was not going down like this.

I wrenched my arm from his grasp and ran behind the sofa, Steven following close behind. I ran to the door and pulled it open. Thankfully, he hadn't latched the deadbolt. Attempting to sprint out into the hallway, I screamed, "Help! Someone help!"

Steven was right behind me. He hauled me inside, slammed the door shut and shoved me away from it. Losing my balance, I fell backwards, my head catching the corner of the coffee table. Sharp pain stabbed into the back of my skull, and all went dark.

I AWOKE BLINDED by the bright fluorescents on my kitchen ceiling. I tried to move, but my hands were bound in front of me with the purple and orange scarf I wear for outdoor catering events. I lay on my back on the cold ceramic tile floor. I tried to lift my head to see what he'd used to tie my ankles together, but pain sliced through my skull as if split with a meat cleaver.

The sound of thudding bowls and jars and the rustling of packages drew my attention toward the commotion. Steven was emptying the contents of my refrigerator and making a horrible mess of my kitchen.

"What are you doing?"

Steven regarded the Styrofoam takeout box in his hand and opened the lid. It was the slice of chocolate chunk cheesecake I'd picked up at the Cheesecake Factory over the weekend. He picked a fork out of the dish drainer, took a taste, and held it out to me. "Pretty good. Want some?"

He held the container under my nose, taunting me. Bastard. I'd been thinking about that cheesecake all day, but watching him now, I didn't think I'd want cheesecake ever again. If there was an ever again.

"Nah." He laughed, shaking his head. He tossed the box over his shoulder into the sink.

"Hey," I yelled. "You're trashing my kitchen." I winced as searing pain bounced inside my head. Okay, no lifting heads and no shouting.

Steven balled up a dish towel and stuffed one end into my mouth. "Quiet!"

My mouth was already dry as day old bread, but this cotton towel would absorb any bit of saliva that was left. I felt like a suckling pig bound up with an apple stuffed into its mouth.

Standing back, he assessed his work then removed all the refrigerator shelves and drawers until it was a big, empty shell. "Let's see," he said, turning the dial. "We'll set the temperature all the way down. The colder it is, the quicker you'll lose consciousness. See? I can be compassionate." He chortled again.

As it dawned on me why he had emptied my refrigerator, I shook my head "no" until the pain felt like it would burst me open. I scooted across the floor away from him, pressing my bare heels into the tile. He laughed, grabbed my ankles and dragged me toward the refrigerator. I'd been in the walk-in cooler the day before, and I had no intention of being put in that situation ever again.

He got behind me and sat me up. First he tried to pick me up by the arms. Then he tried to lift me from the waist. For the only time in my entire life, I discovered a benefit to being overweight. The gag in my mouth suppressed my laugh.

"God damn it, you are one heavy bitch," he groaned. "You're just delaying the inevitable, Trudie. I'm going to get you in there somehow."

Steven squatted next to me on the floor and tried to get me into a fireman's carry over the shoulder. I squirmed and rolled and twisted and kicked my bound feet, aiming for his crotch and hitting my target.

"You fat bitch," he groaned. He dropped me back onto the floor and doubled over, dropping to his knees and then onto his side.

Fat bitch? No one calls Trudie Fine a fat bitch. Once, in the high school cafeteria, when that prissy cheerleader Jenny Jones had called me a fat bitch, I'd knocked her down, sat on her stomach and rubbed my spaghetti in her face. It had been a waste of a good lunch, but no one in school ever called me that, or any other nasty name, again.

Still groaning, Steven started toward me.

My body trembled with anger. He'd threatened me, trussed my body like a turkey ready for the oven, and called me a fat bitch. I'd had just about enough of him.

We were on my turf now: the kitchen. I inspected the room to see what ammunition might be available and pushed my heels into the floor to back myself up to the drawers and cabinets.

Unfortunately, my galley style kitchen is small, and Steven easily grabbed my legs and began to pull me toward him. I lifted my bound hands up above my head and hooked the scarf onto a cabinet handle.

Again, I kicked my feet as hard as I could. Steven emitted a loud grunt as I connected with his face.

He turned onto his back, hands covering his face. Then, slowly, he rolled onto his stomach, lifted his head and sneered at me. Blood spurted from his nose and mouth as a tooth clinked onto the ceramic floor. I congratulated myself for only a moment before I saw the murderous rage in his eyes as he started toward me again.

"You are a dead woman, you fat tub of lard."

I should have been terrified, but his name-calling only fueled the fire in my belly and fed my resolve. I hung onto the cabinet handle and eased myself away from him, scanning the room desperately for some type of weapon.

As Steven crawled in front of the dishwasher, he lifted his head to leer at me. I saw another opportunity. The last time I'd loaded the dishwasher I hadn't completely closed it. I raised my feet and, latching my toes around the rubber gasket on the side of the door, shoved it down as hard as I could on his head. He dropped to the floor, face first.

I didn't wait to see if I'd knocked him unconscious. I just hoped I had time to make my escape. I lifted my hands to detach my scarf from the cabinet door handle, rolled onto my stomach and inched my body backwards past the refrigerator. I trembled to think of Steven attempting to stuff me in there for a slow, cold death.

In my narrow kitchen, I edged past him, pushing against the floor with my bound hands to back out of the room. My heart pounded against the floor so hard that I wondered if he could feel the vibration.

I inhaled a silent, ragged breath and when I had almost reached the exit to the kitchen, Steven, with a great roar, suddenly shot to his feet, rolled me onto my back and pounced on top of me. He put his hands around my neck and began to squeeze, his thumbs cutting off my air passage.

"You're not going anywhere, bitch. You're history."

I struggled beneath him, trying to push him off with my legs and knees. He wouldn't budge. I couldn't breathe. I attempted to inhale through my nose, my only available channel to life. Nothing.

In silence, I cried. I cried for Daniel, maybe my one chance for love and happiness. I cried for Mr. Schwartz and for the college girl I'd never met and even for the general manager who'd run off with Ally's profits. He deserved punishment for his crime, but not the cold, dark death he'd endured.

Steven squeezed harder. Colored lights blinked in the blackness that engulfed me, a sure sign I was losing consciousness. There was nothing I could do but cry for myself.

"Trudie. Trudie." The voice sounded muffled and distant. "I'm here, Trudie."

Daniel? Was I dead already and joining him in the hereafter?

I heard banging and more banging and then a loud crash, wood shattering. Steven was off me. Suddenly I could breathe and was writhing on the floor trying to intake air through my nose and coughing with the gag in my mouth. I opened my eyes and there was Daniel, standing over me in the doorway.

"Trudie," Daniel said, kneeling down to me. "Are you all right?"

Daniel was alive. And he had come for me. I felt the tears well.

He had a deep cut at his temple, and his face was bruised and bloody. His blue blazer was stained and torn at the seams, and his tattered shirt hung half in, half out of his khakis, which were blackened at the knees.

Then I gasped. Steven, who must have hidden himself in another room, stood right behind Daniel, ready to attack. When I spotted him, Steven smiled at me and put his finger to his lips, as if we were throwing a surprise party.

What was wrong with Daniel? A police detective should know how to enter a crime scene. He had completely ignored standard police procedures to get to me. I made my eyes as big as I could and shifted them back and forth between Daniel and Steven. I shook my head and then nodded toward Steven. Just as Daniel finally got the message and started to turn, Steven hit him over the head with a half-empty bottle of Merlot.

Daniel collapsed. Shards of glass and the burgundy liquid splattered everywhere.

"Well, well, well. The boyfriend lives. Sloppy of me, wasn't it?"

Steven stooped down in between Daniel and me and rummaged under Daniel's jacket. "Well what have we got here?" he said, struggling to retrieve the gun from its holster. When he finally wrestled it out and held it up in front of him, I knew from the police shows I watch that it was a semiautomatic. Of course, that's what all cops carry.

"How convenient," he said, glancing at me and grinning again. "I can take care of both of you."

Still kneeling, Steven studied the gun in his hands and stroked it, almost reverently. He examined the pistol as if trying to figure out how it worked and then, lowering his hands, aimed the gun directly at Daniel's head. I groaned, the only sound I could make, and squeezed my eyes shut as his index finger pulled the trigger.

I waited. Nothing. Not a sound.

I opened my eyes. Steven tried again to pull the trigger, but nothing happened. Obviously, he knew nothing about guns, or at least about semiautomatics. I realized that Daniel kept his pistol decocked in its holster. But it would only be a matter of moments before Steven figured out what to do to make it fire.

No. I would not let him do this. A few minutes ago, I thought I'd lost Daniel. But now that I knew he was alive, I wasn't going to let Steven take him, and my chance at happiness, away from me. Steven was still stooped next to Daniel, his back so close, almost touching me.

I saw that he'd figured it out, his thumb on the lever, about to cock the pistol.

He pulled the lever back with his thumb then slowly moved his arm down, aiming the gun at Daniel's head.

I scanned the kitchen wildly, searching for anything I could find to save us. Then I spotted my weapon.

To my right, the dishwasher stood open, the utensil rack within my grasp. With both hands still bound, I lifted them up and over the rack and slid them snugly around the handle of my Santoku. Knowing I had to be quick, I extracted the knife. Then, pushing my elbow against the dishwasher door with all my strength, I rolled myself over and plunged the blade deep into Steven's back.

As if in slow motion, Steven arched his back away from me, throwing his shoulders back as his body went rigid. A stream of blood trickled down the back of his shirt, the rivulet widening across the fabric. As he slumped to the floor, the gun fired with an ear-splitting blast that echoed through the room and caused my ears to ring.

Oh no, I thought. I was too late.

I heard the pounding of footsteps in my apartment, and as uniformed police thundered into my kitchen, guns drawn, everything went black.

I opened my eyes to a bruised, bloody and wine-stained Daniel pulling the gag out of my mouth. "You're alive," I croaked from my parched throat. Then, "I'm alive." I grinned.

"Apparently, you saved both our lives," said Daniel, untying my hands and feet. "With the proverbial 'both hands tied'. Trudie, I totally underestimated you. I guess all those TV cop shows were worth watching after all."

He kissed my wrists where they had been bound and then my mouth. "I was sure I'd be too late," he whispered, his eyes moist.

I giggled, releasing a dribble of tension. "Maybe those shows helped a little. But Steven never should have messed with me in my kitchen."

# Chapter Twenty-Three

Seated beside Daniel on my sofa, I watched as Steven was transported out on a stretcher, EMTs and police officers walking alongside.

I began to cry.

Daniel put his arm around me. "What?"

"I'm relieved that Bradley is alive. If I'd have killed him...I don't know if I could have lived with that. He's young and has his whole life ahead of him." I dabbed at my eyes with the wadded-up tissue I'd been holding for the last hour.

Daniel lifted my chin and glared into my eyes. "That's Steven, remember? Bradley doesn't exist. And he's probably going to be behind bars for that whole life you're so worried about."

"I know. But I'm still convinced there's a Bradley locked somewhere inside. He was a good soul."

The door flung open and Zach burst in. "Trudie, are you okay? I came as soon as I got your message." He sat down on the other side of me, took my hand and leaned his forehead in to mine. "I never trusted Bradley, from that first night he came out of the wine cellar. I can't believe I almost lost you."

Daniel cleared his throat. "Uh, Zach. Trudie's okay. I've got this taken care of."

Zach half lifted himself off the sofa and leaned toward Daniel. "Listen, Trudie is my best friend. If anyone's going to take care of her, it's me."

Daniel tightened his hold on my shoulder. "And I said I've got it covered."

"You're hurting her." Zach was now on his feet.

"Hurting her?" Daniel stood up, too. The air was thick with testosterone.

I held my arms out between them. "Hold on, here. Listen, both of you are special to me." I paused. It was time to let the steam out of the pot. "Daniel, will you leave us alone for a few minutes? Please?"

Daniel hesitated, looking back and forth between Zach and me. "All right. If that's what you want." He joined the other officers gathering evidence in the kitchen.

I turned to Zach. "I have a confession to make. I want to get everything out in the open because I value our honest relationship, and I'm tired of keeping secrets."

Zach cocked his head. "Okay."

"Daniel and I have been…seeing each other. I didn't want to tell you because you were in trouble, and I didn't want to upset you."

"You mean I was in jail and you were dating the guy who put me there? And all the time, I thought that maybe we had something between us?" Zach ran his hands through his hair—not a good sign.

I pulled his hands down and held them in mine. "Zach, you know you are, and always will be, my BFF. We work together every day, and there is no one else in this world I want as my business partner. I love you with all my heart, but taking the relationship beyond that is not an option."

He looked down at his lap.

"Zach." I put my hands on either side of his face and he lifted his gaze to me. "You need to know that in the middle of everything that's happened over the past week, Daniel came into my life."

I locked eyes with him, hoping he could see right through to my soul. "I'm sorry, Zach, but I think I'm falling in love with this man. Well, I'm not really sorry. I know our behavior might be viewed as unethical, and I may not have always been very loyal as a best friend. But I've stood by you a hundred percent in every other way. I hope you'll forgive me."

Zach stared silently at his clenched fists. Then he relaxed and smiled at me. "Trudie, I guess I'm happy you've found love. I put you in a very uncomfortable position. We're a team, bonded together by friendship. It wasn't fair of me to try to insert some kind of romantic relationship where it doesn't belong."

He blinked. "If both of us are being truthful, I should tell you that I've never really gotten over my feelings for Ally."

My heart just about leaped out of my chest. "You still have a thing for Ally? After all these years?"

"I'm afraid so."

I put my hands on his shoulders. "Zach, Ally feels the same way about you."

"What?" Zach shook his head. "No, she doesn't."

"Yes, she does. Bradley, I mean Steven, told me. He said she's always wanted you. He was the one who put peanuts in that girl's food at college. To get rid of the competition for Ally." I squeezed his shoulders and nodded at the disbelief on Zach's face.

"Really? And all this time I thought it was Ally who killed her." Zach shook his head. "I was a real shit to her. Never even gave her a chance. I was convinced she did it." He stood up and began to pace. "How will I ever make it up to her?"

"Zach, you can make it up by being honest with her. Steven's been stalking her for years, supposedly 'watching her back.' And she's been speaking to him on the phone for the past year, baring her soul to him. She cares for you."

"Do you think I should call her?"

"I think you should go see her, talk to her. Find out for yourself."

He hugged me. "Are you okay if I leave now?"

I glanced toward the kitchen and grinned. "I'm more than okay."

Zach beamed as he walked to the door. "I'm on my way."

"Oh, and Zach. Remember, you two still have those plane tickets to Toronto. Maybe the airline will give you guys a credit for the missed flight, or exchange them for a different trip."

He gave me a thumbs up and slipped out the door.

After the police left, I had lots of questions for Daniel and wanted answers. "Okay, what did Steven do to you that he thought you were dead?"

"I was less than a mile away from here when he ran me off the highway into a steep ravine. My car rolled over three times, down the incline and caught fire. What he didn't know was that I was thrown free of the car into the bushes. I must have passed out, but when I regained consciousness I could see him up through the branches standing at the top of the hill, watching my car until it was a burnt shell."

I stiffened as he told the story. "Then he almost did kill you. Oh, Daniel." I wrapped my arms around him, forgetting his cracked ribs.

"Easy, girl," he groaned. "I still have some healing to do."

"Wait a minute. If you were thrown from the car that means you weren't wearing a seatbelt, right?"

"Right, but it did save my life, didn't it?"

"Yes, but why weren't you wearing a seatbelt?

Daniel brushed his knuckles along my cheek. "I was in a rush to get here. I knew you were in trouble and that somehow this guy, Steven Carver, was involved. Our investigation kept zeroing in on him."

"Why? How could you know about him?"

"We tracked his movements. He grew up in Philadelphia but moved to Charlotte when Ally was in school with you. We traced him to a hotel in Maryland the day the college girl died and Chicago when Ally's business manager was found dead in his restaurant walk-in cooler. He's been living in Maryland since Ally graduated, so I went

233

to his apartment to ask questions, but he didn't answer the door. Maybe he knew I was on to him."

I shook my head. "I can't believe he was following Ally all those years, and she didn't even know. But when did you find out that Bradley was Steven?"

"I didn't. Until I saw Bradley watching my car burn. He just stood there on top of that hill, a big grin on his face. I know it's not an excuse for not buckling up, but all I wanted was to get to you before he did."

"Okay. This time it worked out for the best. But in the future, I don't want to worry about you driving around without a seatbelt."

He smiled. "You would worry about me?"

"Of course I would. When Steven told me he'd taken care of you and that you were never coming, I freaked. I didn't know what I'd do without you." I frowned at Daniel. "How did you get here anyway, without your car?"

He laughed. "Trudie, I couldn't get here fast enough. My cell phone was lost in the accident. So I climbed that hill through mud and brambles and vines to get to the highway. But then, no one would stop to pick me up. I probably looked like something out of the Blue Lagoon."

"Well, could you blame them? You're a mess." His clothes were ripped and covered with mud, and his face was smeared with dirt and dried blood. "So how did you get here?" I asked again.

"Finally, the driver of a big rig took pity on me and stopped. I showed him my badge, told him where I needed to be and used his phone to call the station. We were so close, we made it here before the cops arrived."

I leaned against Daniel's chest and put my arms around him. "I'm just happy you got here when you did. I thought I was done for."

Daniel tightened his hold on me and kissed my forehead. I lifted my chin and he kissed my eyelids, my nose, my cheeks and then my lips. "I've got you now, Trudie. And I'm not letting go."

THAT NIGHT IN Daniel's bed, I lay safe and warm in his arms.

"I'm puzzled about something else," I said.

He laughed. "Again with the questions?"

I sat up against my pillow. "What can I say? I won't be able to sleep until I'm satisfied."

He grinned. "After a couple of hours in bed, you're still not satisfied? I guess I'll have to rectify that." He pulled me down and began nibbling at my neck.

"Stop," I shrieked. "That tickles. And I want an answer to my question."

"Okay," he said. "Ask away."

"Bob Lewis. I was sure he had something to do with Mr. Schwartz's murder. You know—the pulverized peanuts in his pants pocket. And he and that guy Mason being so secretive about getting his pants dry cleaned. What was that all about?"

Daniel chuckled. "Trudie, you did some great investigative work, I must say. So I followed up and got a warrant to search the Lewis house."

"You did? You mean you believed me and actually followed my lead?" I grinned at him. "So what did you turn up?"

"I turned up a whole hamper full of pants pockets with traces of pulverized peanuts."

"What? No."

"Yep," he said. "Any pair of pants you'd have taken from that hamper would have had peanut crumbs. It turns out that Bob Lewis is on a low-carb diet."

"Well, I know that. I catered a low-carb dinner at his house. So?"

"So he always keeps a stash of peanuts in his pants pockets for when he wants a snack. Evidently, he'd forgotten Mr. Schwartz was allergic to peanuts and realized too late that he shouldn't have put them in his pocket when he went to the party. He purposely wouldn't shake Schwartz's hand that evening because he didn't want to cause an allergic reaction. That's why Mrs. Lewis thought her husband was acting belligerent and that they were arguing. But it was all very innocent. When Lewis confided to his business associate about it, Mason suggested he get the pants dry-cleaned so he wouldn't be incriminated in his death. And that, young lady, is what you overheard at the Shiva house. Not a plot to cover up a crime."

My mouth was open, and I was speechless for a moment.

"So, I guess Ally actually told me the truth about her relationship with Bob Lewis," I said. "And from what Steven said, she wasn't lying about the college girl who died or the bars for her father or about the trip to Toronto."

Maybe about the abortion, too, I thought. Could it have been

Zach's baby after all?

I shifted my head on the pillow to look at Daniel. "I hope Ally and Zach work this out. I think they'd be happy together."

"Like us?" Daniel asked.

"Yes, just like us." I ran my fingers through his hair and kissed him.

"You know you can stay here as long as you want," he said.

My condo, now a crime scene, would be a mess for a while. Even so, I didn't know if I could ever live there, or face that refrigerator, again without thinking about Steven.

"My parents would love for me to move in with them."

"But I want you here, naked and in my bed with me." He nibbled at my earlobe. "If I could only uncover you," he crooned into my ear.

I'd wrapped myself like a burrito, still self-conscious about my multitude of curves and bulges.

He peeled back a corner of the sheet to reveal my shoulder and breast. "You're beautiful, Trudie."

I closed my eyes and savored the movements of his hands and mouth. "Right now, this is the only place I want to be."

Daniel smiled and moved in for a kiss. "Then you'll stay?" He brushed the hair from my face.

Helping him remove the sheet that enveloped my body, I smiled. "Stay? I barely know you, Detective Goldman."

He shook his head at me. "Will you stop with the Detective Goldman bit? It's Daniel."

"Daniel." I put my hand behind his head and pulled him back

down to me for a long, lingering kiss. "Well, maybe I'll stay for a little while. This is kind of nice."

"I've got you for a little while, then?" He grinned broadly and ran his thumb along my jawline.

"You've got the whole enchilada, baby. The whole enchilada."

Turn the page for recipes from

# A Fine Fix

*Recipe provided by executive chef, James Turner

# Trudie's Knock-Out Sangria*

(Schwartz backyard Mexican Fiesta)

Makes 2 qts or a little more

1 C sugar
1 C water
1 bottle red wine
½ C Triple Sec
½-1 C brandy
½ C tequila
¾ bottle of seltzer (1 liter)
1 orange
1 lime
1 lemon
1 granny smith apple
½ C maraschino cherries (de-stemmed)

Combine sugar and water in small pot and simmer until sugar is dissolved. Let cool. This is simple syrup.

In a pitcher, add red wine, triple sec, brandy, tequila, and seltzer water.

Add simple syrup. Adjust sweetness. You can add more seltzer water to dilute or add more triple sec or sugar for sweetness. (If adding more sugar, make sure it is dissolved by stirring before adding fruit.) Slice oranges, lemon, and lime and cut in half. Medium dice granny smith apple.

Add fruit and cherries to sangria.

Chill in refrigerator for 1 hour.

Serve in wine glass. Make sure to get some of the yummy fruit when serving!

# Mango Salsa*
(Schwartz backyard Mexican Fiesta)

Makes about 2 cups

1 large ripe mango medium diced
½ red pepper small diced
½ green pepper small diced
½ small red onion small diced
1 medium jalapeño pepper seeded and small diced
3 sprigs chopped cilantro
1 tbsp vegetable, canola or olive oil
juice of 1 lemon
juice of 1 lime
salt and pepper to taste

Combine all ingredients in a bowl, cover, and refrigerate for 30 minutes before serving.

# Salmon Fillets with Honey Chile Glaze*
(Schwartz backyard Mexican Fiesta)

4 6-oz portions of salmon
salt and pepper
1-2 tbsp olive oil

**For the Honey Chile Glaze:**
1-2 tbsp olive oil
½ small diced onion
1 tsp chopped garlic
1 tsp Dijon mustard
1 tsp chopped cilantro
¼ tsp paprika
1 chipotle pepper in adobo smashed into paste
¾ C honey

**Glaze:**
In a small saucepan, cook onion and garlic with a little oil until soft. Use moderate heat so garlic does not burn.

With a French knife smash the chipotle pepper with a little salt with the side of the knife blade and add to the onion and garlic.

Add the remaining ingredients. Simmer for 5 min and set aside.

**Fish:**
Brush both sides of the salmon fillets with olive oil and season with salt and pepper. Using a non-stick pan, sear the fish on both sides for about a minute. Transfer to a baking dish. Baste with the honey chili glaze and bake at 400 degrees for 10 minutes.

Serve glaze over top the fillets.

# Grilled London Broil
(Lewis dinner party)

Serves 4

1 flank steak (1 ¼ to 1 ½ lb)
1 tsp salt
1 tsp sugar
1 tsp dry minced onion
½ tsp dry mustard
½ tsp dry or fresh rosemary
¼ tsp ground or freshly grated ginger
1 tsp whole peppercorns
¼ C fresh or bottled lemon juice
½ C salad oil
1 clove garlic, split

Mix together salt, sugar, minced onion, dry mustard, rosemary, ginger and peppercorns.

Add lemon juice. Mix well. Mix in salad oil and garlic.

Place steak in glass container or gallon size plastic bag. Add marinade.

Marinate in refrigerator 3 to 4 hours or overnight, turning occasionally (overnight is best).

Remove meat from marinade and grill about 7 minutes on each side for medium.

Transfer to cutting board and let meat stand for 10 minutes, then slice in thin diagonal slices.

# Flan*
### (Schwartz backyard Mexican Fiesta)

Serves about 8

1 C white sugar
1 tbsp light corn syrup
3 eggs
1 can sweetened condensed milk (14 oz can)
1 can evaporated milk (12 oz can)
1 tbsp Kahlua or coffee flavor liqueur
2 tsp vanilla extract

Preheat oven to 350°.

In a small pot combine corn syrup and sugar. Simmer on medium heat until sugar starts to turn a golden brown (about 8-10 minutes) with only an occasional stir as too much stirring will crystalize the sugar. **This will be hot!** Carefully, but quickly, pour into a round 8-9 inch glass baking or pie dish, tilting the dish to coat the bottom with the caramel.

In a medium bowl combine eggs, sweetened condensed milk, evaporated milk, vanilla, and Kahlua. Mix well with a metal whip or cake mixer. Pour mixture over caramel in the baking dish.

To make a water bath for even cooking: Place the baking dish in a roasting pan. Add hot water to the roasting pan so water comes halfway up the sides of the dish. Be careful not to get any water in the custard mix. Carefully move the roasting pan with the water and baking dish to the oven.

Bake 40-55 minutes or until custard has set. It may jiggle a little when moved.

Remove baking dish and water bath from oven. Refrigerate in baking dish 4-5 hours or overnight.

When ready to serve, run a knife around the inside of the dish to loosen. Place a plate or platter on top and invert flan to pop out.

Top with fresh berries or toasted almonds.

# Ally's Cookie Bars
### (peanuts optional)

¼ lb butter
1 ½ C graham cracker crumbs
1 C flaked coconut
1 pkg (6 oz) chocolate chips
1 pkg (6 oz) butterscotch chips
1 can sweetened condensed milk
1 ½  C chopped walnuts or peanuts


Preheat oven to 350° (325° for a glass pan). In a 9" X 13" pan, melt butter in oven.

Sprinkle graham cracker crumbs over melted butter, mix together and press into pan with spatula or back of spoon. Sprinkle coconut, chocolate chips and butterscotch chips over crumb mixture.

Sprinkle nuts on top and pour condensed milk over entire mixture.

Bake for 30 minutes or until golden brown.

Cool before cutting into squares.

# Acknowledgements

Trudie Fine came barreling into my mind one day in July at a Wildacres Writers' Workshop and wouldn't budge until I began to put her on paper. Since then, she has channeled herself through me onto the page, both of us lovers of food and cooking.

Without the consistent and persistent help and encouragement of my critique groups, Novel Experience and White Oak Writers (WOW), I could not have brought this project to fruition. Heartfelt appreciation to Cindy Young-Turner, Mary Doyle, Mark Willen, Jonathan Allen, Brian Connors, Vic Brown, C. J. Cooper, Alma Lopez, Holly Callen Berardi, Eileen McIntire, Marilyn Greenspan, Rochelle Maya Callen, and Bill LaFond, many of whom are talented published authors in their own right. Thank you also to my beta readers, in particular Blanca Miller and Olga LaFond, whose comments also helped to imprint these pages. I am very grateful to Leonard Spitzer for taking the time to educate me about semiautomatic pistols.

Sincere thanks to my incredible instructors, Ron Rash, Ann Hood, Luke Whisnant, Michael Parker and Nancy Bartholomew, in whose class Trudie Fine was born. These generous and gifted writers gave me the self-confidence to pursue my writing and the guidance to constantly strive to improve my skills.

I was honored that James Turner, an executive chef in Washington, D.C., provided me with such magnificent recipes. Find out more about James and where you can currently sample his fabulous food at www.gdeitchblog.com.

I am deeply indebted to my family, Stanley, Marcie and Matt, who never questioned when I was finally going to publish my book. Stanley, you always encouraged me and never complained about my numerous critique group meetings, writing conferences and my week away each summer. I love you so much for your support.

# About the Author

Gale Deitch enjoys writing all types of fiction—novels, short stories, flash fiction and poetry. Her flash fiction piece, *Prima*, has been featured in the March, 2013 issue of literary magazine, the *Rusty Nail*, and her poetry in the 2011 Maryland Writers Association poetry anthology, *life in me like grass on fire, love poems*. In the fall of 2013, literary magazine *The Writing Disorder*, will feature her short story, *Pressing Matters*.

Although most culinary mysteries take place in small town U.S.A. locales, having been born and raised and still residing in the Washington, D.C. area, Gale's Trudie Fine mystery series, and much of her other writing, is based in her hometown, Washington, D.C.

Gale works for a large non-profit nursing home and senior living system. She has two grown children and lives with her husband in Rockville, Maryland.

Following is an excerpt from the next book in the

Trudie Fine mystery series...

# Fine Dining

coming in 2014

Excerpt from

# Fine Dining

**M**icah followed her into the alley.

She spoke in a hushed voice, but one I could still hear. "I want you out of here now." Then it began to crescendo. "I want you out of my house, out of my kitchen, out of my restaurant, out of this town." Now she yelled at the top of her lungs, her voice strangled. "I want you out of my life—forever. I wish you were never born. Now. Get. Out."

Tears sprung to my eyes. I knew May loved Micah, that he was her only living relative, and even with all his failings, she still believed that one day he would grow up and make something of himself. But seeing her now, disgraced by her brother in front of her staff, her business neighbor, and me, her friend, I knew that all of her hopes and dreams for Micah had disintegrated.

I didn't want her to have to face me now in her embarrassment, so I turned to leave. That's when I discovered Daniel, standing in the doorway. He had seen it all unfold.

As we returned to our table, I glanced up at the other diners who seemed to be looking to us for word about the loud ruckus in the kitchen. Daniel put his hand up and nodded, indicating that all was okay and they could return to their meals. I noticed that the men

Micah had spoken to earlier were gone; two young couples now occupied the corner table.

Daniel signaled Katie to our table for the check. Her entire demeanor had changed, her face drained of all color, her eyes ringed with red. Had she been distressed for May or upset that Micah would be leaving town? Either way, I felt bad for her in her sweet innocence. Katie acknowledged him with a nod and stepped into the kitchen.

And we waited. I was anxious to leave so May wouldn't have to face us. I wanted to get home with Daniel and speak to him about those thugs who were terrorizing local business owners. Most of all, I just wanted to get into bed with him to lay in the comfort of his arms. Where was Katie with that check?

Screams emerged from the direction of the kitchen, muffled at first and then more pronounced, and seeped into the dining room like a noxious gas.

Daniel sprang from his seat and ran into the kitchen.

I followed close behind.

As I entered, tortured cries rang out from the alley. I followed Daniel out the back door. The restaurant staff stood in a ring gazing down at the ground, their shrieks and sobs escaping into the muggy August air.

"Police," Daniel pronounced in an authoritative tone as he urged his way through.

I took advantage of the opening he'd created and peered through to see what had happened. The sight made me gasp. A man's body lay face up, the stain on his white shirt growing larger by the second like a paper towel absorbing a spill. His face was turned away from me, but reflecting from the overhead spotlight on the building, a large diamond sparkled in his left ear.

May sat on the ground rocking back and forth, her voice keening, face to the heavens. Her hands were raised high, grasping a Santoku knife dripping with blood.

Made in the USA
Charleston, SC
17 July 2014